The
Ballygandon
Giants

Also by Gordon Snell

The Ballygandon Giants

Gordon Snell

POOLBEG

Published 2006
by Poolbeg Press Ltd
123 Grange Hill, Baldoyle
Dublin 13, Ireland
E-mail: poolbeg@poolbeg.com
www.poolbeg.com

1 3 5 7 9 10 8 6 4 2

A catalogue record for this book is available from the British Library.

ISBN 1-84223 -284-3
ISBN 978-184223-284-2 (from January 2007)

Cover designed by Steven Hope
Typeset by Patricia Hope in Optima 10.5/15
Printed by
Litografia Rosés, S.A. Spain

About the Author

Gordon Snell is a well-known scriptwriter and author of books for children and adults. Other books in the 'Ballygandon gang' mystery series include *Dangerous Treasure, The Mystery of Monk Island, The Phantom Horseman, The Case of the Mystery Graves, The Secret of the Circus, The Library Ghost, Fear at the Festival* and *The Deadly Camera*. He is also author of *The Tex and Sheelagh Omnibus*. He lives in Dalkey, Co. Dublin, and is married to the writer Maeve Binchy.

To dearest Maeve,
with all my love

1

A Star Guest

"You call yourselves Giants," said Molly glumly, "but the only gigantic thing about that game was the other team's score!"

"Yeah, four goals to one isn't great," said Brendan, "but Dessy and I did our best." Molly, her cousin Brendan and their friend Dessy were trudging back from the football pitch in the park by the river, to Molly's house in Ballygandon. Brendan and Dessy were down from Dublin, staying with Molly's family for a holiday. They had been playing for the Ballygandon Giants, who had just been beaten in the local Junior League match by the Killbreen Cowboys.

"The Giants' goalkeeper is rubbish," said Molly. "I could do it better myself!"

"Of course, you could," said Brendan. "It's ridiculous that girls and boys can't play on the same team!"

"Just you wait," said Molly. "I'll be a star on the Irishwomen's soccer team one day!"

"No problem," said Dessy. "Hey, what do they call it

when two managers are yelling at each other on the touchline?"

"Tell us, Dessy," said Brendan.

"A penalty *shout-out!*"

"You should get a penalty yourself for your bad jokes, Dessy," said Brendan, tripping him up.

"*Foul!*" cried Dessy, and began to wrestle with Brendan.

They were just outside Molly's parents' grocery shop. Her black dog Tina ran out of the door barking loudly, and jumped up and down as Brendan and Dessy struggled. "She wants to join in the game," said Molly, as Brendan fell over and Tina stood on his chest and began licking his face.

"It'll be red cards all round for you lot," said Molly's father, coming out of the shop, "and no tea, either! I was just coming to tell you it's ready."

* * *

While they were having tea, Molly's parents told them someone would be coming to rent a room in the house for a few weeks.

"He's twenty, and he's been living in England most of his life," said Molly's father, "but his family came from round here originally. In fact, he says this used to be his grandmother's house long ago. That's why he got in touch with us to see if he could stay."

"He's recovering from an accident to his leg," said Molly's mother, "and he thought while he's getting better he could stay here and work on an article he wants to write about the area."

"We can tell him a lot," said Molly. "All about the castle and the ghost of Princess Ethna."

"And don't forget the Lough Gandon Monster!" said Dessy.

"He's probably more interested in facts," said Molly's father.

"Oh, that monster's a fact, all right," said Dessy firmly. "Didn't we make it ourselves?"

In fact, the Gang *had* constructed a floating 'monster' which they had shown off at the big regatta on the lake.

"Yes," said Brendan, "but I wouldn't be surprised if there's a real monster down there somewhere in the depths."

"Anyway, we can take him fishing," said Molly. "We'll give him a great time. What's his name, Dad?"

"Michael Cheddar."

"That's a cheesy kind of a name," said Dessy.

"I'm sure you aren't the first one to make a joke about it, Dessy," said Molly's mother.

"When is he coming?" Molly asked.

"Tomorrow morning. Grandpa Locky said he'd bring his car to meet him at the station."

"Great, we'll all go along too," said Molly. "We'll give him a real Ballygandon welcome!"

* * *

They were at the station next day when Molly and Brendan's grandfather Locky arrived in his battered old green car.

"Well, I see the Gang's all here!" said Locky as he got out.

They went on to the platform to wait for the train, and told Locky what they'd heard about Michael Cheddar.

"If he's writing about this part of the world," Locky said,

"he should have a chat with Oliver up at Horseshoe House where I live. He does historical research and he's got lots of old maps and stuff like that."

"We'll bring him up to Horseshoe House some time," said Molly.

"Here comes the train now," said Brendan.

"What does your man look like?" asked Locky.

"I don't know," said Molly, "but I'm sure he'll be looking out for us."

"No mistaking the Ballygandon Gang!" said Locky, as the train pulled in.

There were only half a dozen passengers getting out, and among them they saw a tall young man with curly fair hair, wearing a check shirt and a green jacket. He had a walking stick which he used to help him get down from the train, then he reached back and took a big blue holdall out and put it down on the platform.

He looked around.

"That must be him," said Locky. He waved and called out; "Mr Cheddar?"

The young man grinned and waved back.

"Wow!" cried Brendan. "I can't believe it!"

"What's up?" asked Dessy.

"Do you know who that is?" Brendan said in amazement. "It's the famous footballer, Mickey Mascarpone!"

"Mascarpone?" said Locky. "That's a kind of cheese, too."

Brendan, Molly and Dessy hurried along the platform.

"Welcome to Ballygandon!" said Molly. "I'm Molly Donovan – you're coming to stay at our house."

"Great," said Mickey. "It's good to meet you."

Molly introduced Brendan and Dessy, and then as Locky came up to them she said: "And this is my grandfather, Locky."

"Hello there," said Mickey, shaking hands. "Thanks for coming to meet me."

Brendan picked up the holdall and they walked towards the exit. Mickey was limping as he went, and leaning on the stick.

"Sorry about this," he said, "I got this knee injury, you see."

"Yes, in the game against Newcastle, wasn't it?" said Brendan.

Mickey stopped, and smiled. "You know who I am then?"

Dessy said, in his gangster-style voice, "Yup, Mick, I'm afraid your cover is blown!"

"I did wonder if I could get away with it all right."

"No way," Brendan grinned. "You're famous!"

"And anyway, mascarpone is a much nicer cheese than Cheddar," said Locky. "Come on, let's get you to the car and you can rest that leg."

In the car, Mickey said: "Before we go, could I ask you all to do me a favour?"

"Sure," said Locky, as the others nodded eagerly.

"The reason I used a different name and wanted to spend some time out here in the country was to escape the newspapers. They're really hounding me these days."

"Is it because of Janey Jezzabella, the film star, being your girlfriend?" asked Molly.

"Hey, you seem to know all about me!" Mickey grinned. "Yes, since we split up the tabloid papers are after me the whole time. So I thought I'd try and disappear for a while, and go somewhere I wouldn't be recognised. But it doesn't seem to have worked, does it?"

"We'll keep your secret, Mickey," said Brendan. "I mean, *Mister Cheddar*!"

"The trouble is," said Locky, "if the kids here recognised you, won't other people as well?"

"I suppose they might. I didn't realise I was so well known. I guess people here read the tabloid papers too."

"Yes," said Molly. "Ballygandon isn't the back of beyond, like some people from the city think!" She glared at Brendan and Dessy.

"It's a problem," said Mickey. "I don't want to have to skulk indoors all the time."

"I know what we can do!" said Molly excitedly. "We'll disguise you!"

"Disguise me? How?"

"We can dye your hair black!" cried Molly.

"And give you a false beard," Brendan suggested.

"You can borrow my baseball cap and pull it down over your eyes," said Dessy.

"You couldn't ask anybody to wear that sweaty object!" said Molly.

"Well, let's get you home first, anyway," said Locky, starting the car.

* * *

When they had settled Mickey into his room, he joined them at the kitchen table.

"You know, Michael," said Molly's father, "you look sort of familiar. I wonder where I could have met you before?"

"Maybe on the telly, Dad?" Molly smiled. "Running up and down the soccer pitch?"

"I'd better come clean," said Mickey.

He told Molly's parents who he really was, and why he wanted to stay out of the limelight.

"We're going to make him a disguise," said Molly.

"I must say I thought *Cheddar* was an odd kind of name," said her mother.

"Some people would say *Mascarpone* was even odder," said Mickey. "You see, my dad was Italian, and my mum was Irish, and we used to live in Scotland, in Glasgow. My grandmother lived with us, and she often talked about Ballygandon and the house she lived in here."

"This actual house?" said Molly.

"Yes, she loved it when she was growing up here. She said it was a treasure, a real treasure."

"It's not so much of a treasure just now, I'm afraid," said Molly's father. "The roof needs repairing and the paintwork outside is peeling. We'll sort it out when we can afford it."

"We're doing fine. It's a lovely house," said Molly's mother. "I can understand why your gran was happy here."

"Thanks for making me so welcome," said Mickey. "I'm looking forward to exploring the area. I'm supposed to take a lot of exercise while I'm here, and walk as much as I can, so I can get this knee working properly again."

"We'll come with you," said Brendan. "We can walk up to O'Brien's Castle on the hill right now, if you like."

"Is that the ruin we could see from the road?"

"That's it," said Dessy. "It's haunted. You see, years ago there was this terrible murder, and a princess was stabbed to death with her own brooch –"

"We can tell Mickey the whole story when we're up there," said Molly. She thought *she* should be the one to tell people the history of her own home-town.

"Game ball," said Dessy.

"And talking of game ball," said Brendan, "maybe while you're here you might help us with our soccer training? Then we'll be the stars of the Ballygandon Giants!"

"Well, I'll do my best," said Mickey, "even though I can't do any running myself yet, with the knee and all."

"That's great," said Dessy. "Let's go! We can take a ball with us and show Mickey our moves."

"Your moves are mainly tripping over your own feet, Dessy!" grinned Brendan.

"Yeah, and yours are falling on your backside!"

"Now, boys, stop squabbling!" said Molly. "You see what I have to put up with, Mickey?"

"Even the best teams have arguments," said Mickey tactfully. "Now, are you going to take me on this walk?"

"Sure thing," said Brendan.

"But we haven't got you disguised yet," said Molly.

"I've got an old rainjacket with a hood you could pull over your head," said her father. "I'll get it."

*   *   *

Locky said he wouldn't join them, he had to get back to Horseshoe House, so he waved them off at the gate to the yard in front of the Donovans' shop. Molly and Brendan led the way, and Mickey followed, limping, with the hood of the rainjacket covering his head.

As they walked up the main street of Ballygandon on the way out of town towards the hill and the castle, a Land Rover passed them. They didn't notice that the driver was Seamus Gallagher, who ran the pub in the nearby town of Killbreen. He was up to his neck in all kinds of shady schemes, and had often tangled with the Ballygandon Gang in the past. He was also the Manager, as he called himself, of the Killbreen Cowboys, their arch-rivals on the football field.

As he drove past, he wondered who that most irritating gang of kids had with them. Who was the hooded figure limping along with the walking stick? Seamus decided to try to find out.

2

The Disguise

"They told me to exercise, and this climb will either strengthen my knee or wreck it completely!" said Mickey Mascarpone, as they clambered up the rocky winding path towards the ruined castle. "I think I'll take a rest here."

He sat down on a big rock beside the path.

"You must be hot in that rainjacket," said Brendan.

"Sweating like a pig!"

"I reckon you could take it off now," said Molly. "There's no one up here to see us."

"Except Princess Ethna, and she won't talk," said Dessy.

"Is she the one you said haunts the castle?" asked Mickey.

"That's right," said Molly. Now she had her chance to tell him the legend of Princess Ethna. "She was murdered in the castle centuries ago, on the night before her wedding. She was going to marry the son of the O'Brien chieftain who ruled the region from the castle. But, during the feast that night, she was found dead on the stairs leading up to the top of the tower. She had been stabbed with the big pin of the Celtic brooch she was wearing. That's the tower you can see sticking up out of the ruins." Molly pointed up the hill at the castle.

The ruins looked jagged and menacing against the grey banks of clouds in the sky.

"It looks a spooky place, all right," said Mickey. "What happened after they found her murdered? Did they discover who did it?"

"No, but Ethna's clan accused the O'Briens, and there was a bloody feud between them which lasted for more than a hundred years."

"No wonder she haunts the place. Has anybody actually seen her?"

"Not exactly," said Molly, "but there have been people almost frightened to death by something on the stairs of the tower. And there seems to be a kind of spirit guarding the place. We've often had the feeling it's helping us and giving us messages."

"Lucky you!" said Mickey. "I sometimes feel I could do with a kindly spirit to help me on the pitch."

"I don't think Princess Ethna played football," said Dessy.

"She might have," said Brendan. "I read somewhere that football started way back in history, with rival mobs beheading one of their enemies, and kicking the head around."

"It sometimes feels as rough as that when you're out there playing!" said Mickey. "Well, my knee feels better now – let's carry on up the hill."

Molly's dog Tina bounded ahead of them as they went on climbing up the path.

They showed Mickey around the ruined castle with its

arched, empty windows, and the huge stone fireplace you could stand up in.

"OK, Molly, you're in goal!" cried Dessy, bouncing the football he had been carrying.

"You're on!"

Molly stood in front of the fireplace, as if it was a goalmouth. She shifted from foot to foot, hands out, waiting for the shot. Dessy dribbled the ball towards her, and kicked. Molly jumped to the side and caught the ball easily.

Now it was Brendan's turn. He approached from the right, the ball at his feet. Then he kicked it hard, and once again Molly jumped and caught it.

Mickey was sitting on a stone bench watching. He clapped his hands and said: "You're a great goalkeeper, Molly! You'll play for Ireland one day."

Molly grinned, and told him about her ambition to be a soccer star.

"Well, everyone has to start somewhere," said Mickey, "though I can't think of many players who began their career in a haunted castle!"

They went on roaming among the ruins, with Mickey picking his way carefully over the tumbled stones, so as not to fall and hurt his knee again. They came to the tower with the stairway curving upwards inside it.

"That's where Ethna's body was found," said Brendan.

"The blood was trickling down the stairs," said Dessy. "Oozing like treacle, it was."

"You've got a gruesome imagination, Dessy," Mickey laughed.

"Too right," said Brendan. "It's like his jokes."

As they gazed up the stairway, Molly got out her tin whistle and began to play a slow, mournful tune. It added to the eerie atmosphere of the place, and Mickey shivered.

"I don't think I'd fancy climbing up those stairs," he said. "It would be too dangerous anyway, because of my knee. At least, that's my excuse!"

"We don't mind going up there, eh, Brendan?" said Dessy.

"Not at all," said Brendan. "Why don't you lead the way?"

"After you," said Dessy.

"No, after you!"

"You're a pair of scaredy-cats," said Molly. "I'll go first. Mickey, can you hold on to Tina, please? Don't let her follow." She went into the entrance of the tower and began going up the stairs.

"I'm right behind you, Molly," said Brendan, following.

"I'll stay and keep Mickey and Tina company," said Dessy. "Besides, the stairs might not bear the weight of three of us."

"You're a wise man, Dessy," said Mickey with a smile.

Molly and Brendan went slowly up the winding stone stairway, keeping their backs to the stone wall of the tower. Here and there, narrow windows in the tower gave them a view of the hills and fields around Ballygandon. They could see the park with the football pitch, and beside it the river where they went fishing.

"Careful, Molly," said Brendan, "don't forget the stairs end soon."

"Don't worry." Molly knew that a few steps more would take her to where the stairway had broken and the stones had crashed down on to the ground below.

A step too far would send her plunging down into empty

13

air. She stopped, and clung to the wall, gripping a window ledge with one hand. She could see the end of the stairs, and the long drop down to the ground. She felt a bit dizzy, and turned away.

She looked out of the narrow window.

"Hey, that's odd," she said. "Brendan, take a look at this."

"What's up?" Brendan came up and stood beside her.

"Look over there – you can just see the old road that winds behind Quarry Hill."

"Yes, I can see a yellow truck going along it. I thought that road was closed after the quarry shut down."

"It was. So what's a truck doing there?"

"Search me."

"It's gone behind the hill now."

"Maybe it's something to do with the quarry. Checking the site, or whatever."

"Maybe."

"Hey, are you guys all right up there?" Dessy's voice called from below.

"We're fine!" Molly called. "We're just coming down!"

"We were getting worried," said Mickey when they reached the bottom.

With Tina bounding ahead, they made their way back and out of the ruined castle.

"Better put the jacket and hood on again, Mickey," said Brendan. "We may meet people once we get down the hill."

"Tomorrow," said Molly, "we'll get you into disguise!"

*   *   *

After breakfast the next day, while Mickey lay on the sitting-room floor doing his knee-stretching exercises, they planned the disguise. Molly said she would rummage in the box of Christmas decorations under her bed, where she thought there was a Santa Claus beard they could use. Molly and Dessy would go on a shopping expedition to buy hair-dye and fake-suntan lotion.

Mrs Fitzgibbon who ran the chemist's shop was an inquisitive woman.

"I hear you have a young guest staying with you," she said.

"Yes," said Molly, "he's here to relax while he gets better from a knee injury."

"Tricky things, knees," said Mrs Fitzgibbon. "I've got just the thing for him. It's this heat ointment. Rub it in and it goes right down to the muscles. It worked a treat for my sister the time she fell down the stairs."

"He's got all his medicines from his own doctor," said Molly. "We wanted something else."

"Some suntan lotion for a start," said Dessy.

"Off to somewhere nice, are you? The Riviera perhaps?" Mrs Fitzgibbon eyed Dessy scornfully. She clearly didn't see him as someone you'd find lounging on a fancy Mediterranean beach.

"No, not to keep off the sun, to look as if you've been in it," said Dessy.

"Oh, a fake suntan, is it? Good idea, lad – you do look a bit pasty-faced."

She produced a bottle. "Anything else?"

"We want some hair-dye," said Molly. "Black hair-dye."

Mrs Fitzgibbon looked at Molly's black curly hair. "You're not going grey already, surely?" she asked.

"No, it's for . . . it's for the dog! Her tail's going white."

"Now I've heard everything," said Mrs Fitzgibbon. "Well, I won't say a word to the judges when it wins the prize in the Dog Show!"

* * *

When Molly and Dessy got back, they found Brendan and Mickey waiting at the kitchen table, with a big enamel basin they had borrowed from Molly's mother. They had filled it with water, and put a towel beside it.

"We're ready for the dyeing," said Brendan.

"By the way, I found this in the Christmas box." Molly produced a bushy grey beard with hooks to go over the ears. She handed it to Mickey who hooked it on. The others looked at him and laughed.

"Oh, this will fool them OK," Mickey said. "Especially when I come down the chimney saying HO-HO-HO!"

"You're right, Mickey. It's not going to work," said Molly. "Let's hope the hair-dye will be more successful."

They took the tubes and a small plastic bottle from the dyeing kit, and set to work. Brendan read out the instructions, and Molly poured squirts of dye on to Mickey's head and rubbed it in.

"It smells horrible," he said.

"Don't worry," said Brendan. "It says here the next stage is to wait for a while, then rinse it out."

Eventually Mickey knelt on a chair and slowly lowered his head into the basin of water. Molly splashed the water on to his hair to rinse it. Suddenly, Tina jumped up on to the table, keen to be part of the action. She put her head in the basin and began drinking the mucky water.

"Tina, get off!" cried Molly, pushing her away.

The dog jumped off the table, knocking the edge of the basin so that the water sloshed all over the table and on to Mickey's shirt. Mickey gulped and spluttered and Tina barked happily.

"Grab the towel!" said Molly.

Mickey dried himself and said: "How do I look?" His hair had gone black, but only in patches, so that it looked piebald.

"I think we'll have to have another go," said Brendan. "Let's try the suntan while your hair dries out."

So they poured out some of the suntan liquid into Mickey's hands and he rubbed it into his face. "I'm going to end up looking like a clown," he said. "I suppose I can always find a job in a circus."

Molly's mother came into the room and gazed at the scene in astonishment.

"It's all right, Mam. We'll clear it up!" said Molly.

"I'm sure you will," said her mother sternly. "But I just looked in to say your father called, Brendan. He's coming down this evening to stay for a day or two, for some investigation he's doing around here."

"Grand," said Brendan.

When Molly's mother had left, Mickey asked what Brendan's father did.

"He's a journalist," said Brendan.

"Just my luck," said Mickey with a frown.

3

Treasure on the Map

"No offence to your father, Brendan," said Mickey, "but I came out here to get away from journalists."

"He won't write anything if we ask him not to," said Brendan.

"We don't have to tell him who Mickey is," said Dessy. "We'll have his disguise sorted by the time your dad arrives."

"Of course, we'll have to tell him," said Brendan. "After all, Molly's mother and father know."

"But they don't work for the papers," said Molly. "Your father says he's always looking for good stories."

"Not this kind of story," said Brendan. "He doesn't go in for scandals and tabloid stuff."

"Not so far," said Dessy.

"What do you mean?" asked Brendan angrily.

"Once a newshound, always a newshound," said Dessy.

"Don't talk rubbish!" said Brendan. "You pick up these

words like *newshound* and fling them around as if you knew what you were talking about."

"I do know!"

"You don't!"

"Listen, you guys, there's no need to quarrel," said Mickey. "We'll tell your father who I am and why I'm here. I'm sure he'll respect my privacy, like the rest of you."

"Thanks, Mickey," said Brendan, glaring at Dessy.

"I'll go and get some cleaning stuff from the shop to mop all this up," said Molly.

She went through to the shop which was attached to the house.

There she found Mrs O'Rourke, their old enemy, who owned the holiday caravans, arguing with her father.

"Your kids are kicking footballs around in my field," she was saying. "It's frightening the horses."

"Is this true, Molly?" her father asked.

"No," said Molly, "it wasn't us at all. We don't go near that field – we use the playing field in the park."

Just then Locky came into the shop. He was excited. "Charlie," he said to Molly's father, "I've brought Oliver over from Horseshoe House. You know those old maps he's been studying? He reckons one of them might show that there's some kind of treasure buried right here near your house!"

"We'll go inside and talk about it," said Molly's father. "Goodbye, Mrs O'Rourke. You'll have to find someone else to blame for the footballing in your field."

"You haven't heard the last of this!" said Mrs O'Rourke.

As she went out of the door, she looked at Locky with

interest. She was thinking that, if what he said was true, she'd have to find out more.

*   *   *

Locky and Oliver spread out their maps on the kitchen table, which had now been cleaned and dried after the messy dyeing session.

"Now," said Oliver, "my friend the Professor tells me this map goes back to 1824, before most of Ballygandon was built, but you can see there was a place called that."

"Yes, there it is. I can see the name," said Brendan, "but there's not much else, just a few little black squares, and fields marked out."

"Those would have been farms, part of the big estate of Lord Killbreen. His mansion was where the hotel in Killbreen is now."

"What about the castle? Is that it in the middle of those circular lines?"

"Yes, they mark the hill, and that little network of squares is the castle. It was already in ruins when this map was made."

"And can you see our house?" asked Molly

"It wasn't built then, but you can see where it would be. This line is the road that runs just outside there, and here's the clump of trees at the back, so you're between those trees and the road, just here."

"There seems to be a faint mark there," said Molly.

"That's right. Someone has scratched a little X on the map. There are other X's too, scattered about."

"*X marks the spot!*" said Dessy. "That's what it says on all the pirate maps!"

"You've seen them all, have you, Dessy?" Brendan smiled.

"Of course," said Dessy. "I sailed the seven seas with Long John Silver – *and* his parrot! *Yo-ho-ho and a bottle of rum!* That's what we used to sing, up on the yard-arm. I remember one time in the Caribbean –"

"Stow it, Dessy. We want to hear about the map," said Brendan.

"Well, Dessy's not far wrong in fact, according to the Professor," said Oliver.

Dessy raised a fist in triumph and smiled around at them all.

Oliver turned the map over and pointed to one corner of it. "See there, in tiny writing, it says '*hic gaza est*', with an X after it."

"It sounds like a footballer with hiccups," said Dessy.

Oliver ignored him. "It's Latin. It means '*here is treasure*'. You can see a cross there in the middle of the castle. That must be where the Ballygandon Hoard was found a few years ago."

"Haven't people dug for treasure where the other crosses are?" Brendan wondered.

"I believe they have, but nothing's been found as far as we know," said Oliver. "The Professor says some of them may have been put there to mislead people, so they wouldn't know which marked the real treasure."

"Hey, maybe that's why Tina was digging in our yard the other day!" said Molly.

Molly's mother laughed. "I wish it was, but that was definitely a big bone I gave her. She was burying it."

21

"I've just thought of something," said Mickey. "You know I told you how my grandmother was always saying this house was a real treasure? Maybe she meant there *was* real treasure, buried here. She may have heard old stories about it."

"I think we ought to get digging!" said Brendan.

"We can't dig up the whole yard," said Molly's father.

"Anyway," said Oliver, "if it's there at all, it could be underneath where the house is now."

"Wouldn't it be great if we found another Ballygandon Hoard?" Molly was excited.

"Then we could certainly afford to get the roof fixed!" said her father.

Oliver was doubtful. "I'm not sure it would belong to you officially. There are all kinds of rules about who owns treasure trove, as they call it."

"We'll sort that out when we find it," said Locky. "I reckon you'd certainly deserve a cut, if it's on your land. If you could spare me a gold coin or two, I could put it on a horse and win us a fortune."

"Like you did on the Irish Derby last time, Dad?" laughed Molly's mother.

"That was just some bad advice I got," said Locky.

"Anyway, we've got to find the treasure first," said Molly.

"If it's still there," said Oliver. "Someone might have dug it up long ago, even before your house was built."

"Don't be such an old misery boots, Oliver," said Locky. "I'm sure it's still there. All we've got to do is find out where."

Brendan looked at his watch. "It's time we got down to the

park for the team practice. It would be great if you could come, Mickey, and give us a few tips."

"I'd be glad to," said Mickey. "I guess I'd better wear the rainjacket and hood, just in case, though it'll make it hard to see what's going on."

"I think we could risk it," said Brendan. "After all, your hair is already a different colour."

"Several different colours, in fact!" Mickey grinned.

"You could go into show business," said Dessy, "and star in *Joseph and the Amazing Technicolour Hairstyle!*"

"The dyeing was a bit patchy," Molly admitted. "But I've just thought of something else. Why don't you wear sunglasses?"

"It's an idea, but I haven't got any with me."

"I've got a pair somewhere," said Molly's mother. She rummaged about in a drawer and produced a pair of sunglasses with pink glittery frames. "I got them that time we went to Spain on holiday."

Looking a bit doubtful, Mickey put them on. The others laughed.

"No danger you'll be noticed, wearing those!" said Locky.

Outside, Locky put the map on the back seat of his car. He was going to drop Oliver off in the town to visit a friend, then drive the rest of them down to the park for the football practice. They offered Mickey a lift, but he said he'd better walk, to get the exercise.

* * *

23

In his glittery sunglasses on a grey day, Mickey got some curious glances from the players as he sat on a wooden rail at the side of the pitch. And Molly got some muttered comments when Brendan brought her on to join the practice. But she was so much better than most of them that they didn't do anything – and besides, they knew they would have Brendan and Dessy to deal with.

During a break, the three of them came over to Mickey.

"You all did very well," he said, "and you really showed the rest of them up, Molly.

"Any advice, Mickey?" Brendan wondered.

"Hold my stick, would you, Locky?" Mickey took a few limping steps on to the pitch. "I think my knee is bearing up OK."

Dessy rolled a ball towards him. Mickey gingerly pushed it with his foot, then began to dribble, stumbling a little. But they could see just how expert he was. He showed them his footwork, and then passed the ball to Brendan, and they all had a go.

"It looks so easy, I could almost do it myself." Locky stepped forward and gave the ball a kick. "Ouch!" he cried. "That ball must be made of wood!"

There was a further practice session, and Brendan, Molly and Dessy tried to use the moves Mickey had showed them. He congratulated them.

"The Ballygandon Giants will win the trophy yet!" said Brendan. "Just wait till our Cup Final match against Killbreen on Saturday!"

"It's time I picked up Oliver and got back to Horseshoe

House." Locky turned towards the car parked on the road. "Hey, who's that rummaging in the back of my car?"

They all looked at the car, and saw the back door open, and someone leaning in over the back seat.

"It's Mrs O'Rourke!" said Molly. "She's looking at your map!"

4

Dogs and Newshounds

"Hey! That's my car!" Locky shouted, as they all went towards it. "What do you think you're doing?"

Mrs O'Rourke emerged from the car, looking flustered.

"Oh – sorry," she said. "I was . . . er . . . I was looking for my dog."

Molly frowned. "I didn't know you had a dog, Mrs O'Rourke."

"Didn't you? I just got him the other day. He ran off and I can't find him. I thought he might have climbed into your car."

"Through the closed doors?" Locky was frosty.

"Oh, it was open, believe me."

"What kind of dog is he?" Molly knew Mrs O'Rourke was making it up.

"Oh . . . er . . . a Scottish Terrier."

"What's his name?" Brendan wanted to know.

"Mac! That's it, Mac!"

"Well, you'll hardly find him on that map you were peering at so closely," said Oliver.

"I thought he might have got underneath it. Anyway, I must be off. I'll just have to go on looking for him."

"Well, if we see 'Mac' we'll let you know." Molly was sarcastic.

"Thank you." Then Mrs O'Rourke noticed Mickey. Forgetting she was supposed to be searching for the dog, she looked at him curiously. "We haven't met. You must be the young man who's staying with the Donovans?"

"That's right. I'm Michael Cheddar. I'm doing some research for an article I want to write about this area."

"Well, you must come and see me. I can tell you a lot about what goes on around here."

"And about some pretty shady goings-on too," Brendan muttered.

Mrs O'Rourke glared at him.

"Thank you," said Mickey quickly.

"I hope you have some luck finding 'Mac'," Molly smiled.

"Mac? Oh . . . yes, the dog. I'm sure he'll turn up. Goodbye for now."

"And good riddance," said Dessy, as Mrs O'Rourke strode away.

* * *

That evening Brendan's father arrived from Dublin while Mickey was out walking to exercise his knee.

"Dad, have you ever heard of someone called Mickey Mascarpone?" Brendan asked.

"Of course, I have. He's that footballer there was all the fuss about, when he split up with his girlfriend, the film star."

"That's him. Well, we've got a surprise for you."

"What's that?"

"He's staying here, in our house!" Molly said in excitement.

"Here?"

"Yes, it turns out that his grandmother used to live here, a long time ago. He hurt his knee and he wants a place to recover, out of the way."

"That's why he's got a false name, Michael Cheddar," said Brendan. "His story is that he's writing an article about Ballygandon and this area. You see, because of all the publicity, he wants to escape from . . . well, people like . . ."

"People like me? Journalists?" Brendan's father smiled.

"That's right," said Dessy. "*Newshounds,* as you call them."

"Well, *I* don't actually call them that, Dessy, but I know what you mean."

"You won't give him away, Dad, will you?"

"His secret is safe with me. I'm not that kind of a newshound. That sort of scandal-mongering is for the tabloid lads."

"Muckrakers, eh?" said Dessy, who liked to think he was a master of up-to-date slang.

"Exactly, Dessy," said Brendan's father. "But funnily enough, it *is* a kind of muck that brings me down here. I'm investigating some of the illegal waste-dumping that's going on. They say someone's running quite a racket in it, somewhere in this area."

"Well, if you need any help, Dad, the Ballygandon Gang is ready!"

"Oh, I know you are, and I'll be very glad of your help. Anything you can find out about hidden dumps or strange trucks carting rubbish could be very helpful."

"We're on your case, Mr O'Hara!" Dessy declared.

"Hey, Molly," said Brendan, "remember that truck we saw on the old quarry road? The road we thought was closed. Maybe that was carrying illegal waste."

"Yes, let's go up to the castle tomorrow and see if we can see anything else."

"That's the kind of sleuthing I need," said Brendan's father. "I'll come with you."

Just then, Mickey came in. They introduced him, and Brendan's father reassured him that he'd keep the secret. He looked with interest at Mickey's piebald hair.

"That's part of the disguise Molly and the gang dreamed up for me," said Mickey.

"Well, I think the Molly Donovan Hairdressing Salon has done an amazing job."

"Hey," said Dessy, "what did the hairdresser say to the guy in the chair?"

"Tell us, Dessy," Brendan sighed.

"I'm just *dyeing* to change your hair colour!"

"At least my knee has improved more than Dessy's jokes," Mickey said. "I think I might soon be able to kick a ball properly again."

"Does that mean you'll have to go back?" Brendan asked.

"Oh, I don't plan to go back for a good while yet," said Mickey. "I'm having such a good time here. Besides, I want to wait to see the Ballygandon Giants win the Cup."

"Good, that means you could be here till next Christmas!"

said Dessy. "Only joking!" he added, as he saw the others glaring at him.

*　　*　　*

That evening at Horseshoe House, they had just finished their meal when Oliver was told he had a visitor, a historian who was doing research about the Ballygandon area. He went off to the sitting room, taking the maps which Locky had brought back to him.

After ten minutes, when Locky had finished his coffee, he thought he would investigate. Who was this historian who had suddenly turned up?

Locky went to the door of the drawing room and listened.

Inside, he could hear Oliver saying: "Well, certainly that cross mark there is where the Ballygandon Hoard was discovered, so there is a chance that some of the other crosses show the location of other treasure."

"And what about this one here?" It was a woman's voice. Locky thought it sounded familiar.

"Oh, that's at the place where Donovans' Grocery is now, but it's not marked precisely enough for us to know exactly where it indicates. It could be near the house, or even underneath it."

"Couldn't a metal detector find it?"

"Well, it depends what it is . . . "

Now Locky recognised the voice. He opened the door of the sitting room.

"Oh, hello, Locky," said Oliver. "This is –"

"We already know each other." Locky was cool. "Good evening, Mrs O'Rourke."

"O'Rourke?" Oliver was bewildered. "But you said your name was Professor Merriman."

"That's my pen name."

"Really?" said Locky. "For all those books you write about horse-drawn caravans?"

"What on earth is going on?" Oliver was getting irritated.

"I hope the 'professor' can explain," said Locky. "She was burrowing around in my car this afternoon, trying to get a look at that map of yours. So now you've had a proper look at it, Mrs O'Rourke, perhaps you'll be on your way, and stop bothering my friend Oliver with all this professor nonsense."

"I've no wish to stay and listen to your rude remarks," said Mrs O'Rourke. She turned to Oliver and said: "Thank *you*, anyway, for being so helpful and courteous, unlike your pal here. Goodbye." She stomped out of the room.

"What was all that about, Locky?" Oliver asked.

"That one is up to no good, you can bet on that. She's after that treasure, I reckon."

"We don't even know there's treasure there, and anyway, what can she do about it, short of bulldozing the Donovans' house?"

"I wouldn't put it past her!" Locky laughed.

*   *   *

"That was Locky on the phone," said Brendan later that evening. "He says Mrs O'Rourke has been up at Horseshoe

House, pretending to be a professor, and trying to find out more about the treasure and the crosses on the map."

"What's all this about treasure?" asked Brendan's father.

They told him about Oliver's research and the map with a cross where the Donovans' house now stood.

"Another Ballygandon Hoard!" Brendan's father exclaimed. "That would be a sensational story."

"It's all a fantasy, if you ask me," said Molly's father.

"Who knows? Right now it's not hidden treasure I'm on the trail of, but hidden waste dumps."

"And the Ballygandon Gang will be following that trail first thing tomorrow," said Molly.

5

Quarry Search

Next day, Mickey set off on a long walk to get his knee exercised, while Brendan's father drove the Ballygandon Gang towards the castle. They parked at the bottom of the hill and took the winding path that led up to the ruins. They made their way over the rock-strewn ground towards the tower. They gazed up the curving stairway inside it.

"Those stairs might not bear three people," said Dessy, "so why don't your father and I stay down here, Brendan? We can keep watch while you and Molly spy out the lie of the land."

"Thanks, Dessy," said Brendan's father, looking quite relieved. "Besides, I'm heavier than the rest of you. Be careful, won't you?"

"We will, Dad." Brendan began to go up the stairway, with Molly following. They came to the window slit from where they had seen the trucks on the roadway down below.

"No sign of anything," said Brendan.

Molly looked too. "But we did see them," she said, "and if we're lucky they'll come again."

"I'll have my camera ready, just in case," said Brendan. He put the camera on the ledge of the window and looked into the lens, pointing it at the part of the road they could see.

They waited for several minutes, then Molly cried: "Look there!"

Through the camera, Brendan could see a yellow truck snaking along the road. He pressed the button. "Got it!"

The truck moved out of sight behind the hill. A few minutes later, another one followed.

"We've got a sighting!" Molly called down the stairs.

"Good work!" said Brendan's father.

Brendan and Molly came down the stairs, and Brendan showed the others the pictures in his camera.

"There are the trucks all right," said his father. "Can you see what they're carrying?"

"I'll see if I can zoom in on the truck. Yes, you can see better now. It looks like black plastic bags in that one. And in the next one, let's see. It looks like broken bricks and rubble."

"They could well be on their way to a dump," said Brendan's father. "But where would it be?"

"How about the quarry?" said Molly. "It stopped working a while ago and they closed it up. No one goes there any more, and there are notices saying *NO DUMPING* and *DANGER, KEEP OUT!*"

"Worth the risk, maybe, for illegal dumping. It seems people will pay quite well to get rid of loads of rubbish. How do we get to the quarry?"

"The main entrance was on the road up into the hills," said Molly.

"Well, let's get into my car and you can show me the way."

They drove out of town and up a winding road where the rocky hills on either side sloped steeply down towards them, covered with yellow patches of gorse. Here and there a sheep stood grazing by the roadside. They rounded a bend and came to a big gap in the hills on the left. There was a high fence of upright black steel girders across the gap, with a massive pair of gates in the middle. There was a big wooden sign on the gates which said: GANDON QUARRIES. The paint on it was dusty and peeling.

Brendan's father drove off the road on to the gravel beside it, and stopped in front of the gates. They all got out. The gates were covered in a wire mesh which was frayed and rusty. They were held together by a heavy metal chain, fastened with a large padlock. The chain and the padlock were rusty too.

Brendan took hold of the chain and rattled it. "It doesn't look as if anyone's opened these gates for a while," he said.

"There's no sign of any new tyre tracks, either," said Molly.

"And no sign of anyone being here," said Brendan's father. "That hut just inside there must have been for the gatekeeper." They looked at the wooden hut. The door was hanging open at an angle, with one of its hinges broken. Beyond it they could see a rusty old broken-down tractor. The place looked totally neglected.

"If I could climb up on to the top of the fence," said Brendan, "I might be able to see further in."

"You can stand on my shoulders," said Dessy. He gripped

the fence and put his legs apart to steady himself, and Molly cupped her hands together. Brendan put one foot on her hands and pushed himself up. Keeping hold of the fence, he got his other foot on to Dessy's shoulder, then hauled himself up.

"I can see down that track that goes behind the rocks there," he said, "but there's no sign of activity. Wait a minute! I *can* see something moving, way over in the distance. It's yellow. Yes, it must be one of those trucks. I'll get out the camera."

As he reached into the pocket of his anorak, he began to wobble a bit on Dessy's shoulders.

"Careful, Brendan," said Molly. "Here, I'll hold on to your ankles." She gripped his ankles while Brendan held on to the fence with one hand, and with the other raised the camera. He looked through it and clicked. Then he began to lose his balance, and the camera slipped out of his hand. Molly dived and caught it before it hit the ground. Brendan began to topple, and jumped off Dessy's shoulders, landing in a heap beside Molly, who held up the camera in triumph.

"See what a star goalkeeper can do!" she cried.

"Bravo!" Brendan's father applauded. "You're a great team!"

Brendan scrambled to his feet. "Let's see what's in the camera."

Molly handed it to him.

"Look!" he said, peering into it. "You can just see the yellow truck in the distance – and it's tipping up."

His father took a look. "That's dumping, no doubt about it. And I guess they're using the quarry. But they're not going through this gate, that's for sure. There must be another way in."

"That road we saw from the castle must lead to a back way into the quarry," Brendan said.

"I thought they'd closed that road." Molly was puzzled.

"Not for dump trucks, it seems," said Brendan, "and if *they* can drive on it, so can *we!*"

"Then let's get going," said his father, heading for the car.

* * *

They drove back into Ballygandon and to the bottom of the castle hill, then took the old road that led round to the back of the hill. It was a country road with patchy tarmac, and a line of grass growing down the middle of it. Straggling hedges shut it in on each side. They drove along for about a kilometre, then saw a wooden gate ahead of them, blocking the road off. A sign on the gate said: *ROAD CLOSED*.

Brendan and Dessy got out and examined the gate. There was just a latch on it but no chain or lock. They pulled it open and the car drove through and stopped. Molly got out too, and the three of them looked at the road near the gate.

"There are muddy tyre tracks here all right," Brendan said, "and very recent ones. This must be the road those trucks were taking."

They pushed the gate shut again, and the car drove on. The road went through a valley, and they came to a gap in the hills at one side.

"Could you stop, Dad?" said Brendan. When the car stopped, he pointed through the gap. "See up there? That's the tower of the castle. This is the part of the road we saw from there."

"We're going the same way as the trucks did, then. Let's carry on." Brendan's father drove on, and the road twisted and turned between high hedges and trees.

After another kilometre, they saw a wooden fence blocking the road, and a notice that said: *DANGER! ROAD ENDS.*

"That's weird," said Molly. "We haven't seen any sign of the quarry yet." Once more they got out. They went up to the fence and looked over it. Then they stood back nervously.

"When they say *ROAD ENDS* they really meant it!" said Brendan. Beyond the fence a steep slope of tumbled rocks went straight down into the valley below. At some stage the road must have crumbled away, maybe washed away in a rainstorm. It certainly couldn't have been used for a very long time.

"No trucks have gone past here, anyway," said Brendan's father, "but if this *is* the road they were on, where have they got to? I didn't see any turn-off or junction on the way here, did you?"

They all agreed the road had led directly here. There was nowhere for any kind of vehicle to go off it.

"There must have been some kind of track or gate we missed," said Brendan's father. "We'll just have to turn back and go slowly till we spot it."

He turned the car and they drove back the way they had come, scanning each side of the road carefully. They could see no gap or gate or turn-off at all.

After a while, Brendan's father stopped the car just before

a bend in the road. "This is about halfway back to the gate," he said. "We're all agreed there's no way off the road so far?"

"None at all," they all said.

Suddenly Brendan shushed them, his finger to his lips.

"What's up?" whispered Molly.

"I thought I heard the sound of an engine."

They all listened. Sure enough, from somewhere not far ahead of them, came the sound of a vehicle. Then it stopped. They heard voices.

"OK, open it up."

"Right."

"Hurry!"

"Give me a chance, will you?!"

Brendan said: "Could you wait here with the car out of sight, Dad? Then Dessy and I will creep along round the bend in the road and see what's going on."

"OK, but be careful."

"We will."

Brendan and Dessy crept forward till they could see the road ahead. They crouched down behind a boulder.

"We've found it, Dessy!" whispered Brendan. "The hidden entrance!"

6

The Hidden Entrance

As Brendan and Dessy looked at the two-metre-high tangled hedge of bushes and ivy that lined the road, they saw a gap appear in it. Then a section of the whole hedge swung outwards. They could see that it was really a big metal gate, with wire mesh stretched across it. The bushes and the ivy were twined into the mesh, so that from the outside the whole gate looked like a high, thick hedge. No wonder they had passed it in the car without realising there was an entrance here.

Brendan got out his camera and took a picture of the scene, as two men in overalls pulled the gate open. One of them beckoned, and a yellow truck came slowly out on to the road and stopped. Inside the gate, another truck was waiting. One of the men at the gate went over to it, got in and drove it too out on to the road.

Waiting till the other man turned away from him to push the gate shut, Brendan stood up on the boulder. He could see into the trucks.

"Watch out, Brendan!" said Dessy urgently, as the man closed the gate and turned.

Brendan ducked down again. "Those trucks are empty now," he told Dessy. "They've dumped the stuff we saw them carrying." He took another picture. Then they crept back round the corner to tell the others what they had seen.

"Now we know where the entrance is, we can get in ourselves and take a look at the dump," said Molly.

"We'd better wait till the trucks leave," said Brendan's father. This time Molly crept around the corner and crouched behind the boulder. She saw the man at the gate making sure it was shut, then he went to the second truck.

"OK, let's go!" he said, and climbed in.

Both the trucks revved up and moved off down the road, and out of sight.

"All clear," said Molly, coming back to the others.

They left the car where it was, and moved cautiously towards the hedge where the gate was. "It's cleverly disguised, all right," said Brendan's father, as Brendan showed him where the opening was. "But at least it looks as if they haven't put chains and padlocks on this."

Molly pulled some of the greenery aside. "It's fastened with a piece of sliding metal, like a farm gate," she said. "If I reach through the ivy here, I'll be able to slide it back. There!"

"We'll take hold of the wire mesh through the leaves, and pull it open," Brendan said.

He and Dessy and Brendan's father tugged, and soon the gate swung back a little way. One by one, they edged through the gap.

"We'd better pull it closed again, so no one will know

we've got in," said Molly and she helped the others pull the gate shut, then slid the metal bar back in place.

"Now, let's follow the tyre tracks," said Brendan, leading the way.

* * *

The muddy road led up a slope for a hundred metres, then rounded the corner of a rocky cliff.

"There it is. The dump!" cried Molly in triumph.

They all stopped. They were a few metres from the edge of a great hole. This must be where the rocks had been dug from the quarry. Now the gap they had left was like the crater of a volcano, and far down below them they could see a mass of junk – black plastic bags, old tyres, bricks and slabs of concrete and builder's rubble. There were twisted bits of bicycles, metal tanks, drainpipes, whole doors and even an iron bedstead.

Seagulls cawed and circled, and swooped down to peck about in the mounds of rubbish.

Brendan was busy with his camera.

"Good work," said his father. "We'll have all the proof we need. Now we've got to find out who's organising all this."

"Hey, listen!" said Molly suddenly. "I think I heard an engine."

Sure enough, they could hear the sound of a truck in the distance, over towards the road. It stopped.

"There must be another truck coming in," said Brendan. "They've stopped to open up the gate."

Indeed, after a pause, they heard the engine start up

again. Behind them, round the corner, the truck was approaching.

They wouldn't be able to get back to the gate without being seen. They looked around wildly for a place to hide.

"Quick! Over there!" said Brendan's father. He pointed to the left, where there was a rocky slope near the far end of the ledge which overhung the dump. They could see an old, rusty wagon, once used for carrying rocks from the quarry. It was tipped on its side, with the bottom and the wheels facing out towards them. They all rushed across to it, and crammed in behind it. The wagon shielded them from the road and the trucks coming in from the gate.

They were just in time. A heavily laden yellow truck was lurching and grinding towards them on the muddy track. Through some rust holes in the bottom of the wagon they could see the truck stop and turn, backing towards the edge of the quarry dump. A man in overalls, like the men they had seen earlier, got out and walked towards the edge. He beckoned to the driver of the truck, which backed further. Molly thought it could easily slip in the mud and tumble backwards into the dump. But the first man called out: "Stop!" Then he lugged a slab of rock across and put it behind one of the back wheels.

Brendan put his camera lens into one of the holes in the wagon, and took pictures as the man called "OK!" and with a screech of metal the back of the truck slowly tipped up. Rubble and piles of black plastic bags slid down and tumbled with a crash over the edge and into the quarry below.

"Can any of you see any sign of an owner's name on that truck?" Brendan's father asked.

"I can't, not even when I zoom in with the camera," said Brendan.

"I've written down the licence plate number," said Molly. "It's local to this county."

"Well, that narrows it down a bit," said Brendan's father.

"Can't we follow in the car when the truck leaves?" Brendan wondered.

"It's risky," said his father. "If they spot us, they could turn violent. I don't want to put you lot in any more danger! This is bad enough!"

"Yeah, we'd better not blow our cover," said Dessy.

"I've got an idea," muttered Brendan. He whispered in Molly's ear.

"I'm on for it, if you are," Molly whispered back.

"What are you two up to?" Brendan's father was suspicious. "Don't do anything rash, will you?"

"You know *us*, Dad!"

"Exactly, that's what bothers me."

They watched as the truck lowered itself again. The man standing at the quarry's edge went and climbed in beside the driver.

"Now's our chance!" Brendan pocketed his camera.

"Let's go for it!" said Molly.

They both dashed from their hiding-place towards the back of the truck.

"Brendan! Molly!" hissed Brendan's father, but they were already at the truck.

Molly cupped her hands, and Brendan put his foot out and leaped up, on to the truck. He leaned over the back and managed to pull Molly in beside him, just as the truck began to move off.

It went down the road towards the gate in the hedge, which had been left open. The truck moved out on to the road and stopped. One of the men got out to close the gate.

Brendan and Molly crouched down. "Here, we can hide under this!" said Molly, dragging at a sheet of canvas lying in the back. They pulled it over them. They heard the scrape of metal as the gate catch was shut, then the man got back in and the truck door slammed.

As the truck moved off, Brendan and Molly smiled at one another and gave the thumbs-up. They poked their heads out from the canvas and Molly said: "Phew! It stinks in here!"

She looked out of the back of the truck in time to see Brendan's father and Dessy peering cautiously out of the hedge gate. She gave a wave and the thumbs-up sign.

"They're dare-devils, that pair! Now we *must* follow them," Brendan's father told Dessy. "They could be in danger. Let's get back to the car."

"Don't worry, Mr O'Hara," said Dessy, as they moved off. "Brendan and Molly are on the ball. They can look after themselves. They're the Ballygandon Gang after all!"

"It's the gang they may be tangling with that worries *me.*"

They followed the road through the hills, keeping well behind the yellow truck. They pulled up when they saw it stop at the wooden gate that blocked the road. When it had gone through, they followed.

"Quick as you can, Dessy!" Brendan's father leaned out of the driver's window as Dessy struggled with the gate.

"No problem!" Dessy opened the gate, then shut it again after the car drove through. He jumped back into the passenger seat, calling: "OK, Chief, follow that truck!"

They rounded a bend and saw the road stretching ahead. There were one or two cars, but no sign of the yellow truck. They followed the road till it came to a crossroads. Brendan's father pulled up and they peered down the roads left and right. There was no yellow truck in sight.

"It looks like we've lost them," said Dessy. "We'll just have to go back to Molly's and hope they'll call."

"Brendan's got a mobile," said his father. "Maybe we should call him on that."

"That might really blow their cover," said Dessy. "Best to wait. He might be able to get a text message to us."

* * *

The truck trundled along the road. Brendan and Molly peered out over the back of it, keeping low so the driver wouldn't spot them in the rear-view mirror.

"We're on the Killbreen road, by the look of it," said Brendan.

Sure enough, they soon spotted a signpost which said: *KILLBREEN 2 km.*

The truck went into the town. It rattled over a bridge and then along the river, till it turned down a sideroad. It turned into a gateway where there was a big yard with two or three other yellow trucks parked in it. Then it stopped.

"We'll lie low till they get out," whispered Brendan.

He and Molly pulled up the canvas so they couldn't

be seen. They heard the door slam shut and the men get out.

As their footsteps moved away they heard one of the men say: "We deserve a pint after that."

"It's thirsty work, that's for sure," said the other.

Molly whispered to Brendan: "I think I know just where we are!"

7

Spies

Across the yard beyond the trucks there was a big stack of metal beer barrels, and a skip full of empty bottles. They stood behind a big grey building. On the side, painted in large black letters, were the words: *GALLAGHER'S BAR AND LOUNGE.*

"It's Seamus Gallagher's pub," said Molly. "So now he's into illegal dumping!"

"No surprise there," Brendan grinned. "He's been into most other illegal activities in the past."

"Yes, and we've caught him out in a lot of them."

They remembered other battles the Ballygandon Gang had had with Seamus, and with his frequent partner-in-crime, Mrs O'Rourke.

"I'll take some pictures to show the trucks in the pub's yard."

They climbed out of the truck and went over to the far side of it, where there was another pile of metal barrels. They crouched behind it. Between two of the barrels there was a slit where Brendan poked his camera lens.

"Got it!" he said, pressing the button. He showed Molly the picture in the camera. They could see the back of one of the trucks, with the licence plate clearly visible, and beyond it the side of the pub with the sign for *GALLAGHER'S BAR AND LOUNGE*.

"Stay back. There's a car coming," said Molly. They watched as a sleek black car stopped in the yard. A man in a dark grey suit got out. He had sleek brown hair and a clipped moustache. Brendan thought he looked like a businessman. He went across to the door at the side of the pub and knocked. He looked around carefully, as if he didn't want to be noticed. The door opened and they saw Seamus Gallagher inside. He shook hands with the man and they went in – but not before Brendan was able to take another picture.

"Just in case it could be useful," he said.

"It's a fair bet that, whoever Seamus is meeting, there's something shady going on."

"I'd better let Dad and Dessy know where we are," said Brendan. "Maybe they'll come over and collect us." He started to tap out a text message on his mobile.

"They'd better not come here," said Molly. "Seamus might get suspicious if he saw them."

"I'll say we'll meet them at the bridge." He sent the text. After a short while, his phone buzzed.

"That was quick," said Molly. "They must have been waiting for us."

They read the message: *OK. See you soon.*

"It will be a while before they get here," said Brendan. "Let's go over and see if we can find out more."

They went across the yard to the back of the pub, where there was a window. Kneeling on a barrel, they were able to peer in, past some bottles that were on the window-sill.

Inside in the bar they could see the men in overalls sitting at a table drinking pints. Seamus himself was behind the bar in a corner, and the man in the suit was sitting on a bar stool opposite him. Their heads were huddled together, as though they didn't want the rest of the men to hear or see what they were at. In fact, the man in the suit was passing an envelope across to Seamus, who opened the top of it and flicked through the contents. He was counting.

"Bank-notes, I guess," said Brendan, "but it's a lot of money to pay for a drink!"

"Yes, indeed! Cash for favours, more likely. It could have something to do with the dumping."

Just then, they saw the man in the suit look towards the window. He frowned, and said something to Seamus, who looked across.

It was time to leave.

Molly and Brendan jumped down from the barrel and ran across the yard and out of the gate into the road. They didn't stop till they reached the bridge. They ran across it and crouched down, looking over the river. There didn't seem to be anyone pursuing them.

But they were relieved to see Brendan's father's car approaching along the Ballygandon Road.

*   *   *

Back at Molly's house, they put Brendan's pictures on to the computer and printed them out.

"That's damning evidence, all right," said Brendan's father. "It links Seamus and his trucks with the illegal dumping, which we've seen with our own eyes. Now if we can discover who that fellow is who's paying Seamus, I could have the story sewn up and ready to go into the paper."

"He may not be the only one," said Molly.

"You're probably right," said Brendan's dad. "There could be a whole bunch of people paying Seamus to get rid of their rubbish."

Mickey came in, back from his exercise, and they told him about their adventures.

"This place is full of excitement," he said. "I'll find life dull when I go back."

"You're not going just yet?" Brendan was anxious.

"Oh no, I plan to see the Ballygandon Giants win the Cup first. And I might be able to help you more with training now. My knee is practically cured. Come on. I'll show you."

They went out into the yard in front of the shop, and began kicking the football about. Molly stood against the fence where they had painted the shape of a goalmouth. Mickey dribbled the ball towards her, as if he was going to aim for the left side of the net. Then he switched to his other foot and kicked for the right side. Molly was too quick for him. She also switched and dived for the ball, catching it with her arms outstretched and falling to the ground.

"Bravo!" said Mickey, applauding. "You really are a star, Molly! We'll have to get you in goal for the match."

"Some hopes," said Molly. "The junior teams in this league have never been mixed."

"Well, maybe now's the time to start," said Mickey. "Where are the League Rules?"

"They're up on the noticeboard in the clubhouse down by the pitch."

"I don't remember seeing any clubhouse down there," said Mickey.

"It's that big shed where we change," said Brendan. "They like to call it a clubhouse – it sounds grander!"

"Let's go down there and have a look."

* * *

Inside the big wooden shed there was a square area with a table and a couple of chairs, as well as a shelf with some papers and books piled on it. There were framed photographs of teams on the walls. Through a door they could see a changing room which took up the rest of the building. It had a row of metal lockers along each wall, and in front of them some long benches. Stretching down the middle of the room there was a long rack with hooks on each side of it. On some of these, football shirts were hanging. There were a few boots scattered under the benches, as well as a couple of footballs.

"Welcome to the clubhouse!" said Brendan.

Mickey looked into the changing room, then around the small entrance area. "Well, it's not very luxurious, but you probably have more fun playing the game than some teams with much more glamorous buildings."

"We'll have fun beating the Killbreen Cowboys on Saturday!" said Brendan.

"Let's practise the chant!" said Dessy.

"Oh, you have a chant? Then let's hear it."

"OK, lads, let's go!" cried Molly. "One! Two *Three!*"

And all of them shouted together:

"GANDON, GANDON, BALLY-BALLYGANDON!
GEE – GEE – GEE – GEE, GIANTS!"

"Ferocious!" Mickey exclaimed. "That should have them quaking in their boots. But we can't have you just chanting from the sidelines, Molly – we must get you on the team. Now, where are these League Rules?"

"There's a notice on the back of the door," said Brendan.

Mickey went over and studied it. "Here it is – *JUNIOR LEAGUE.* There's a lot of finicky stuff about numbers and maximum age, and the time for each half, and rules for substitutes and so on. But I can't see any rule where it says girls can't be on the same team as boys."

"Let's go for it, then!" said Brendan. "Molly in goal!"

"Even if it's OK in the rules, there's another snag," Molly frowned.

"What's that?"

"Bruiser Callaghan."

"Who's he?"

"The regular goalkeeper for the Giants. He lives up to his nickname too. He's a desperate bully. Most of the team don't rate him that much, but they are a bit scared of what he'll do if they don't let him play in goal."

53

Gordon Snell

"Well," said Mickey, "we'll just have to show them that Molly's better."

"How can we do that?" asked Dessy.

"I know a way!" Mickey was excited. "We'll have a Penalty Shoot-out!"

"Nice one, Mickey!" said Brendan. "There's a team practice tomorrow. We can do it then. I'll text him with the challenge. He can hardly say no, without seeming to chicken out. I won't say who you are though, Molly."

"I'd better get practising," said Molly. "Will you fire a few shots at me, Mickey?"

"Sure thing."

On the pitch, Mickey and Dessy kicked balls at Molly in the goal, while Brendan got busy with his texting. Then he joined in too. Molly leaped and dived, saving almost every shot that was directed at her.

Brendan heard his mobile buzz, and went to the side of the pitch. They heard him laughing as he looked at the mobile screen. They stopped playing.

"What's the news, Brendan?" Molly went across to him.

"It's a reply from Bruiser Callaghan," said Brendan, "but I'm not sure I ought to show it to you, Molly – you might be shocked by the language."

"Give it here!" snapped Molly, snatching the mobile. She read the message, and laughed too. "Wow! We've really got his back up!"

The others read the message, and Mickey said: "However much he swears and curses, you were right, Brendan – he's taken up the challenge."

"He's sure he'll win, of course," said Molly.

"Then we've got a surprise for him," said Mickey.

A car drew up beside the pitch. Locky got out and called across to them. He was agitated.

They went over to him and asked what was wrong.

"It's Oliver's map, the one with the treasure crosses," said Locky. "We think it's been stolen!"

8

Treasure Hunters

"What do you mean, Locky, you *think* it's been stolen? Where was it?" Brendan asked.

"In Oliver's room, he thinks. You see that's the problem. He isn't sure that's where he left it. It may have been in the sitting-room, or he may have put it away somewhere for safety."

"It's not very safe if he can't remember where he put it," said Dessy.

"I know, I know, that's what happens when you get older, you see. But anyway, we can't find it, and we've hunted high and low at Horseshoe House."

"If it *has* been stolen, I bet I know who took it!" said Molly.

Brendan and Dessy chorused together: "Mrs O'Rourke!"

"Should we go to the Guards?" Mickey suggested.

"The trouble is, we're not sure," said Locky, "and if it turns up we'll look like proper eejits."

Brendan agreed. "Anyway, Mrs O'Rourke would deny it,

and the Guards aren't going to start issuing search warrants just on our say-so."

"We need more evidence," said Molly.

She didn't realise just how soon they were going to get it.

They all crammed into Locky's car and he took them home, then said he'd drive on back to Horseshoe House and help Oliver hunt for the map. They said goodbye to Brendan's father who had to go back to Dublin.

"Time for some more shooting practice before tea!" said Molly.

They went into the yard and shot more balls at Molly in the goalmouth. This time her dog Tina decided she'd join in the game, and began leaping at the ball each time Molly did.

"We'd better not bring Tina tomorrow," said Dessy. "She'd mess up the penalties."

"Take no notice of him, Tina," said Molly. "You'd be better at saving shots than Bruiser Callaghan."

"Hey, what did they call the prizewinners at the Dog Show when the tent caught fire?" asked Dessy.

"Yes, Dessy, what?" Brendan sighed.

"*Hot dogs!*"

* * *

They were all sleeping well that night after the energetic exercise, including Tina, who was lying on the rug in Molly's room. It was after midnight when Molly was woken by Tina, who gave a low growling sound, then another. The dog jumped up on the chair by the window and tried to peer out, with her ears pricked up. She growled again.

"What's the matter, Tina?" Molly got out of bed and stood beside the dog, stroking her head. She looked out of the window. There was a big gravel yard at the back of the house, with a large, ramshackle wooden shed at the far side, where Molly's father kept his grocery van, and stored boxes of supplies for the shop. Behind the fence that ran round the yard there were trees at the edge of a small wood.

Molly was surprised to see a beam of light among the trees. It moved to and fro, and then shone steadily on the fence. It must come from a powerful torch, she thought.

Suddenly, she saw what must have alerted Tina: the head of a large fierce-looking dog, poking through the slats of the fence. Then she saw the bulky figure of a man clumsily straddling the fence, then jumping down into the yard, where he lost his balance and fell over. As he got to his feet, she could see him drag the dog under the bottom slat of the fence by his lead.

Someone else must be holding the torch. She saw the man reach out and take it, then help the other person over the fence. Molly could see it was a woman with her hair tucked into a headscarf. The man reached back over the fence and produced a spade. They stood together in the yard, muttering to each other and pointing. One of them was pointing at the house, the other at the shed. The dog decided to make for the shed, and dragged the man across. It began to snuffle around on the ground near the shed.

Then the woman took the torch, reached into a satchel she was carrying, and pulled out a roll of paper. She opened it out and went across to the man. She gave him the torch and he shone it on to the paper.

Molly realised with a shock that it was the map. So Locky

was right, it *had* been stolen, and there was the thief right out there looking at it: Mrs O'Rourke! And no doubt the figure with her was Seamus Gallagher, with his unpleasant large Alsatian dog, Lonnigan. They were clearly on a midnight treasure hunt. It was time to alert Brendan and Dessy, so that the Ballygandon Gang could tackle this together.

* * *

Molly, Brendan and Dessy crept down the stairs and went to the back door. They decided not to wake Mickey, or Molly's parents, who might want to confront the intruders, or call in the Guards. They held a whispered Council of War, and decided it was best for the moment to observe what Mrs O'Rourke and Seamus were up to. That way they'd have more evidence and eventually be able to catch them red-handed.

So Molly put Tina into the kitchen and shut the door. The dog would certainly give them away if she came out and met Lonnigan. She was already growling and snarling. Luckily no one else in the house had woken.

Carefully, they opened the door. They crouched down behind the tumbledown dog-kennel that stood beside the door. It was originally meant for Tina, but the dog had long since decided that her rightful place was inside the house with Molly, so the kennel stayed there unused.

"If we come out from here to get closer, they'll spot us," whispered Brendan.

"I know, let's edge along the wall and climb over the fence into the wood," said Molly. "Then we can dodge in among the trees till we're at the fence just behind them."

Slowly, step by step, they moved towards the fence. Soon they were over it, and among the trees. They crept along in the shadow of the trees until they could see over the fence near the shed. Lonnigan was snuffling around near the base of the shed wall. Then he started scrabbling at the ground with his paws.

They were near enough to hear what Seamus and Mrs O'Rourke were saying, even though they spoke in hushed voices.

"You see, he's found something!" said Seamus.

"Since when has that dog been able to sniff out treasure?" Mrs O'Rourke scoffed.

"You wait and see," said Seamus, as Lonnigan went on digging. "I gave him a sniff of a silver spoon before we came out, so that he'd get the idea of what he was after."

Brendan and Molly could hardly suppress their laughter at the idea that a spoon would put Lonnigan on the trail of treasure.

But just then, the Alsatian stuck his nose into the hole he had dug, and brought something out, snuffling and growling with delight and wagging his tail.

"Good boy! Good boy!" cried Seamus.

"What's he got?" asked Mrs O'Rourke. "Let's have a look, before he swallows it." She shone the torch on Lonnigan.

"Give it here, there's a good boy," said Seamus, reaching out his hand.

Lonnigan growled, then seemed to start choking. He dropped his trophy on the ground. The torch beam shone on a huge, dirty knuckle of bone. Seamus snatched it up and stared at it.

"Stupid dog!" Mrs O'Rourke's snarl sounded almost as fierce as the dog's. "That's some treasure!"

"That must be one of Tina's bones," Molly grinned. "She's always burying them and then forgetting where she put them."

"I told you we should bring the proper gear," snapped Mrs O'Rourke. "Now we'll have to come back. We can't dig up the whole yard."

At that moment there was a frantic noise of barking, and Tina leaped out of the kitchen window and into the yard.

"Oh, no!" groaned Molly. "I didn't realise the window was open!"

Tina ran straight at Seamus and began to jump up at him, snapping.

"Take it, you horrible cur!" said Seamus, throwing the bone down.

Tina grabbed it, but then with a snarl Lonnigan snapped at Tina, fighting for the bone. Seamus tried to pull him off, dragging at the lead.

"Let's get out of here!" said Mrs O'Rourke. She clambered back over the fence, followed by Seamus, who managed to drag Lonnigan through the fence. Molly, Brendan and Dessy shrank into the shadows of the trees, as man, woman and dog hurried past them through the wood.

"What's going on?" They heard Molly's father's voice, and saw him looking out of a window of the house. They saw Mickey's head too, peering out to see what all the noise was.

"It's OK, Dad!" called Molly, as she clambered back over the fence into the yard, followed by Brendan and Dessy. "There were intruders in the yard but they've run off!"

Molly knelt down and patted Tina, who was happily lying on the ground and gnawing at her re-discovered bone. The outside light went on, lighting up the yard. Molly's father came out of the house, followed by Mickey, while her mother put her head out of the window.

"Are you all right?" she asked anxiously.

"We're fine, Mam. Tina scared them off."

"And look what they left behind!" said Brendan. He bent down and picked up the map which Mrs O'Rourke had dropped in her hurry to get away.

"You're a brave bunch," said Mickey admiringly. "You too, Tina!"

"We're the Ballygandon Gang!" said Molly.

9

Secrets and Plans

In the kitchen, Molly's mother made a pot of tea and produced some of her home-made brack. She watched with a smile as they all munched on it gleefully, including Mickey.

"This is great!" he said.

They unrolled the map. They had decided not to wake Locky by ringing him in the middle of the night. They would tell him about the map in the morning.

"Look, those thieves have put a red mark on the cross where our place is," said Molly. "This was their target all right."

"They've got a nerve," said Molly's father. "What did they plan to do? Dig up our whole backyard?"

"Well, they certainly brought a spade with them," said Brendan, "*and* Lonnigan!"

"And that's what woke Tina," said Molly, stroking the dog's head.

"Do you think they'll come back?" asked Mickey.

"I doubt it," said Molly. "I think we scared them off."

"Well, I'm sure they won't be back tonight," said her mother. "It's time you were all back in your beds."

"Yes, you need your energy for the football tomorrow," said Mickey.

As the Gang climbed the stairs together, Dessy said quietly to Molly: "Do you really think they'll be too scared to come back?"

"That pair? They'd take any risk if they smell a chance of money. They'll come back, no doubt about it. And when they do, I've got a plan that will really scare them off!"

* * *

Next morning when Mickey went out for his walk, they rang Locky.

He was delighted to hear about the map. "I'll tell Oliver right away, and then I'll drive down to see you. I can't wait to hear all about your night adventures. Well done, Ballygandon Gang!"

Once again they studied the map on the kitchen table.

"It's just as well the Ballygandon Hoard has already been found," said Brendan, pointing at the castle on the map. "They would have made even more of a ruin of it, digging there."

"The castle, that's what gave me the idea of how to deal with them next time," said Molly.

"What do you mean?" Dessy asked.

"Mrs O'Rourke is really scared of ghosts, even though she says she doesn't believe in them. If we make her think the treasure buried here is Princess Ethna's, she might think twice about taking it."

"I doubt it," said Brendan. "As you said, that pair would risk anything for money."

"But supposing she saw the ghost of Princess Ethna protecting it?"

Brendan wasn't persuaded. "We may be in the Friends of Princess Ethna Club, but it's going to be hard to get her to come and do a haunting for us."

"Then we'll get someone else to do it for her."

Brendan and Dessy stared at Molly.

Brendan muttered: "*You!*"

"Who else?" said Molly, giving a mock, sweeping bow. "Meet the Ghost of Donovan's Grocers!" She raised her arms and swooped down on Dessy, grabbing him by the neck and giving a crazy, bloodcurdling laugh.

"Let go!" he cried. "I give in."

Brendan was laughing. "It's a crazy idea, but it might work."

"You scared *me,* that's for sure." Dessy rubbed his neck. "When do you think they'll come back?"

"My guess is tonight, and they may bring extra help."

"What, a whole gang of people?"

"No, not people. Equipment. Remember, Mrs O'Rourke said they should have brought the right gear with them? I think she meant metal detectors."

"Metal detectives?" Dessy grinned. "You mean, like a robot Sherlock Holmes?"

"You're an eejit, Dessy," said Brendan. "Molly said metal *detectors*. Those gadgets you push over the ground like vacuum cleaners. They give a buzz where there's metal buried."

"I know *that*!" Dessy scoffed. "I was just joking."

"No time for jokes, Dessy," Molly was brisk. "Now, here's my plan for the haunting . . ."

Their planning was interrupted when Locky arrived, overjoyed to see the map back. He gazed at it and frowned. "The vandals! They've put their own red mark on it."

"That's to show which cross is their target, Grandpa," Molly explained. "But we saw them off, thanks to Tina."

They told Locky all about the adventures of the night. He praised their bravery, but warned them to be careful. "Those crooks are ruthless, you know. They might be back to try again."

"We're sure they will be," said Brendan, "and we'll be ready for them, won't we?"

"Sure thing," said Dessy, "and so will Princess Ethna!"

Locky looked puzzled.

Molly glanced at Brendan, who nodded.

"Grandpa," said Molly. "Can you keep a secret?"

"My lips are sealed," said Locky.

"Then we'll tell you about our plan."

* * *

When Mickey came back from his morning exercise walk, he suggested they did some more goal-shooting practice in the yard, ready for the big penalty shoot-out that afternoon.

Locky smiled. "I'd be happy to help, Mickey, but my trainer has told me to rest up, ready for the next league match."

"We'll do our best to manage without you, Locky."

"Good luck, Molly. You'll stun them!"

"Thanks, Grandpa."

In the yard, Molly defended brilliantly, as the others directed shots at her in front of the painted goalpost.

They had put Tina on her lead and tied it to the gate. She sat watching their game and giving the occasional bark of encouragement.

Then they heard a voice say: "Good dog, good dog!"

They stopped as they saw a man in a suit come into the yard and bend down to pat Tina, who wagged her tail.

Mickey turned away and bent to pretend to adjust his shoes. There was always a risk he might be recognised.

"She's a very friendly guard dog," said the man, patting Tina again.

"Just as well," said Molly, "or no one would get into the shop."

"Good morning," the man said. "I was hoping you sell cigarettes here?"

"Sure," said Molly, "my father's in the shop, he'll help you."

"Thank you," said the man. "Enjoy your game."

He went into the shop.

Dessy was about to kick the ball again, when Molly called urgently: "Brendan! Did you see who that was?"

Brendan said: "Yes, I did. It's the man we saw in the pub with Seamus Gallagher."

"It's definitely him," said Molly. "Look, that's his car, out in the road."

Indeed, there it was, the sleek car they had seen drive into the yard of Seamus's pub.

"Thank goodness he didn't recognise us," Brendan was relieved. "He glanced our way when we were looking through the pub window."

"Now's our chance to find out more about him. I'm going into the shop."

"Be careful, Molly," Mickey said.

"I will. I'll just hang about pretending to stack shelves or something."

She went into the shop.

"Hi, Dad," she said. "I forgot to arrange those cereals you wanted stacked on the shelf."

"Oh – thanks, Molly." Her father looked puzzled.

Molly went behind the counter and knelt down, putting cereal packets from a box on to one of the shelves. Her father was handing a packet of cigarettes to the man over the counter. The man handed him a note. Then he pulled a small brochure from his pocket and gave it to Molly's father.

"Can I leave you one of these?" he asked. "They're some very desirable houses on a smart new estate I'm building just outside Killbreen. Your customers might be interested."

"I'm sure they would be," said Molly's father, looking at the brochure. "I'll leave this here on the counter."

"Thank you. Here's my card." He was just handing over the card when there was a shrill sound, like the first few bars of a song. The man reached in his pocket and produced his mobile. He looked at the screen, then put the phone to his ear and said sharply: "Yes, what is it, Seamus?"

Molly looked up, startled. It must surely be Seamus Gallagher.

The man with the phone listened, and didn't look at all

pleased. He snapped: "Yes, I did get your message, and no, I'm not going any higher!" There was some crackling chatter from the other end of the phone, then the man said: "Listen, Seamus. I can't talk here. Hold on. I'm going out to the car!" He glowered at the phone and mouthed some insulting word, then turned to Molly's father and said: "Thanks, keep the change. Excuse me."

"Thank you," said Molly's father as the man strode out of the shop, with the phone clutched in his hand.

Molly got up and said: "I'll be back in a minute, Dad."

She went out into the yard and saw the man with the phone walk quickly out of the gate towards his car.

Molly said to the others: "Go on playing, I think he's talking to Seamus Gallagher. I'm going to crouch down behind the fence near the car and see if I can hear."

The man got into his car and closed the door. Molly hurried over and crouched down by the fence. The car was just on the other side. Fortunately the driver's window was open, but in any case the man was talking loudly and angrily enough to be heard even down the road.

"You've got a damned nerve, Seamus, trying to up the price at this stage! . . . No, I am *not* going to pay it . . . We had a deal about dumping my rubbish and now you're going back on it. It's no go, I tell you. The deal's off!"

There was a long pause. Molly thought the man had ended the call, but then she heard him say, even more angrily than before: "The trucks? No, you *can't* hang on to the trucks. They're *my* trucks. What do you mean you'll make sure I don't find them? Don't you try any tricks with *me,* Seamus! I'm warning you. Goodbye!"

Watching from the yard, Brendan and the others saw the man glaring at the mobile as if he was going to fling it through the windscreen. Then he slammed it down on the seat beside him, and started the car.

Molly stood up as the car roared away down the road.

Molly told them everything she had heard. Then she went into the shop, and asked her father if she could borrow the brochure and the man's card, to show to the others.

"Sure," her father smiled. "Are you thinking of buying a few houses, Molly?"

"I'm practising to be a tycoon, Dad!"

Outside, they all looked at the brochure and the card.

"*Luxury town houses in a country setting,*" Brendan read. "They look like posh houses all right. Look at this: *Ultra-modern kitchen, two bathrooms, patio, built-in barbecue, Jacuzzi . . .*"

"I could do with a nice Jacuzzi bubble bath," said Molly.

"Hey," said Dessy, "do you know who the Jacuzzi's named after?"

"Tell us, Dessy," said Brendan.

"*Jack Hughes,* of course!"

"If we ever have one, I'll push you under, Dessy."

"Never mind Jack Hughes – it's Damian J O'Regan we need to keep track of," said Molly. "See, that's the name on the card he gave Dad."

Brendan copied down the name and address in his notebook, and took a picture of the houses in the brochure with his camera.

"I think there's someone else we should keep track of, first," he said. "Seamus Gallagher. Let's get Locky to drive us to his pub and see what he's up to."

10

The Mystery Goalkeeper

"This Seamus seems like a busy guy," said Mickey, as they travelled towards Killbreen in Locky's rattly old car. "He's got this scam going on with the dumping, and he's hunting for your treasure in the middle of the night. I'm surprised he has time to run a pub at all."

"It's a fairly grotty pub," said Brendan. "It's mainly a base for Seamus to run his devious schemes from."

"He runs the Killbreen Cowboys team too," said Molly. "At least, he calls himself the Manager."

"Not a lot of scope for criminal activities in that, I suppose," said Mickey.

"Not criminal, perhaps, but he's certainly ready to cheat as much as he can to get the team to win."

"We'll have to watch him then when it comes to Saturday's match," said Mickey.

They got Locky to stop the car just beyond the bridge, then left him to mind it while they walked cautiously along the road to the corner where Gallagher's Bar and Lounge was. They went through the gate into the yard at the back, where Brendan and Molly had hidden in the truck. There were a few cars parked there, but no sign of any of the yellow trucks.

"I wonder what he's done with them," said Brendan.

"So will Mr O'Regan," said Molly. "Look, here's his car now. Duck!"

They saw the sleek car come into the yard. They all ducked down behind a parked van where they couldn't be seen. Molly peered over the bonnet and saw Damian J O'Regan get out of his car. He slammed the door shut behind him and went striding across to the side door of the pub. He didn't stop to knock, but opened the door and went in.

"Molly and I know a spot to spy from," said Brendan. "Mickey, it's best if you and Dessy wait here."

"OK, but take care."

Molly and Brendan went across the yard and climbed up on to the metal barrels beside the back window of the bar. Once more they peered through the plants on the window-sill. Once more they saw Seamus behind the bar in the corner, and Damian J O'Regan opposite him across the bar. This time they could hear Damian's angry voice through the window.

"OK, for the last time, Seamus, what have you done with those trucks?"

They saw Seamus raise his hands in a shrug, and then turn away. Damian put out his hand and grabbed his coat sleeve, pulling him back. He held on to the coat and raised his other hand, clenched into a fist.

Seamus stared straight at him and said: "Hit me if you want, but you won't get the trucks till I get the money."

"You're not getting it."

"Suit yourself. In any case, if things work out, I may not need your money. I'll have a fortune of my own."

Damian lowered his fist. He was interested. "What are you on about?"

Seamus smiled and put his finger to his lips. "It's hush-hush. But if you're good to me, I might cut you in."

"You're raving, Seamus, that's what. You should be locked up. And if I don't get those trucks back, I'll see that you are."

Seamus laughed. "Oh, calling the Guards, is it? Yes, I'm sure they'd be delighted to know all about your payments for rubbish removal."

"I'll give you till tomorrow, Seamus," said Damian. "After that, you're in real trouble." He turned and marched out of the bar, slamming the door. They saw him get into his car and drive out of the yard.

Molly and Brendan were about to climb down from their perch when Molly said: "Wait!"

Watching through the window, they saw Seamus lean down and take something out from under the bar. It was a long black canvas case like a travelling golf bag. They saw him prop it against the bar, and unzip the top of it. He pulled at something inside and took it partly out of the bag. He stood admiring it with a grin. It looked like the metal handle of some instrument, and it had a dial of some kind near the top.

Just then, a customer came into the room and went up to the bar to order a drink. Hastily, Seamus slipped the instrument back into the bag and stowed it back under the bar. He started to serve the drink. Now Molly and Brendan climbed down and went across the yard to tell the others what they had seen.

As they walked back along the road to join Locky at his car, Brendan said: "Do you know what I think that was, in the case? A metal detector!"

"I agree," said Molly, "and if it was, we could be seeing it in action before very long!"

* * *

That afternoon, Locky drove them to the football pitch in the park. In the changing room, the boys in the team were putting on their togs and boots. Brendan looked up as the door opened. A burly figure stood in the entrance. It was Bruiser Callaghan.

His appearance matched his name. He was overweight, with big, bulging shoulders and a thick neck. His red football shirt looked too small for him, as it stretched across his chest. He had a pudgy nose and thick eyebrows, and his red hair stood up spikily on his head.

A silence fell on the room. Everyone looked at the figure in the doorway. Brendan went on tying his boots, and glanced up. "Hi there, Bruiser! How's it going?"

"Down the drain is where *you'll* be going, mate," said Bruiser. "You've got a nerve, challenging *me*! This Mystery Goalkeeper you're bragging about – it's *you*, isn't it?"

The others looked at Brendan with interest. "Oh no," he said, "I wouldn't dare challenge you, Bruiser."

"Well, who is it, then?"

"Wait and see." He went across to the doorway and stood in front of Bruiser. "Now, if you'll just let me past, I'll go and see how my Champ is getting on."

"Champ, that's a laugh!" Bruiser sneered. Some of the others chuckled fawningly. Bruiser came into the room and Brendan went past him, outside to the pitch.

*   *   *

In a corner of the field, Locky stood watching as Molly, Dessy and Mickey kicked a ball about. Then Molly did some stretching and bending exercises to warm up. Brendan came over to them and said: "Bruiser's in the changing-room, throwing his weight about as usual. I haven't told him yet who our Champ is."

"Boy, has *he* got a surprise in store!" said Dessy.

Molly grinned. "Don't you mean '*Girl,* has he got a surprise in store'?"

"Game ball, Molly!" said Dessy.

"Here they come!" Brendan pointed towards the changing room as the team began to come out and on to the field.

Mickey decided he had better put the hood up on his jacket, just in case. The players started to pass balls to each other, running up and down.

Then Bruiser came lumbering out of the changing-room door. He looked across to them: "OK, Brendan, tell your guy to get ready. I'm going to put in a bit of practice."

Bruiser stood in the goalmouth, while some of the others fired shots at him. A lot of the shots were from two or three of Bruiser's cronies, deliberately easy so that he could show off, making totally unnecessary dives and leaps to catch the ball.

When one of the players who was no friend of Bruiser's directed a powerful shot at goal, Bruiser jumped and missed. Sullenly he picked up the ball from the back of the net and kicked it hard at the player, who stepped neatly aside, saying: "Temper, Bruiser, temper!"

Bruiser took a couple of steps towards him and said: "Shut your face, Gary!"

"Who's going to make me?" Gary scoffed.

Bruiser was about to have a go at him, when Rick the Captain called out: "Come on, Bruiser, we're here to play football, not have a punch-up!"

"OK, but I'll see to you later," Bruiser told Gary, stepping back into the goal.

After another five minutes of practice, Bruiser took the ball and began bouncing it. He shouted over to Brendan's group: "OK, I'm ready. So where's your pathetic challenger?"

"Right here," said Brendan.

He and Molly walked across the field and stood in front of Bruiser.

"It *is* you!" Bruiser sneered. "Well, that really is pathetic!"

"No, not me," said Brendan. "Molly."

"What?!" Bruiser stared at them in amazement.

"Hi, Bruiser," said Molly. "I'm ready to roll, if you are."

"You've got to be joking," Bruiser said. "Molly? She's a girl!"

"What a keen eye you've got, Bruiser," Dessy grinned. "Imagine you noticing that! And we always thought you were a bit of a thicko!"

Bruiser took a step towards him, fists clenched.

Molly stepped between them. "Calm down, lads. Well, Bruiser, do you accept my challenge or not?"

Bruiser could think of nothing to say. He just stood there staring, with his mouth open. Finally he snapped: "This is barmy. Girls can't play on the team."

"Why not?"

"It's against the rules."

"OK, show us where it says that in the rules. They're on the notice board inside."

"Fair enough," said Rick the Captain. "Come on. We'll go and take a look."

"This is stupid!" grunted Bruiser. "I'm not taking any more of this nonsense."

"Then come and show us the rule," said Molly.

"Get stuffed!"

Rick went with Molly and Brendan to look at the list of rules. He read them carefully and then said: "You're right. There's nothing in there to say that girls can't play on the team."

They went back to tell Bruiser.

"I don't give a damn what the rules say," said the goalkeeper. "I'm not playing in any team with girls in it!"

One of Bruiser's cronies said: "That's right. You tell 'em, Bruiser!"

But then Gary asked, in a pleasant voice: "You're not chicken, are you, Bruiser?"

"No, I'm damn well not!"

There was a pause. No one moved. Then a voice from somewhere in the watching group said: "*Chook-chook-chook!*"

Bruiser went red in the face and snarled: "Who was that?"

"Never mind, Bruiser," said Rick. "But we're all getting a bit bored here. We'd like to get on with the team practice for Saturday's match. So let's get the penalty shoot-out over, shall we? Unless you want to give Molly a walkover, of course."

Bruiser stood there, looking as if he was about to explode. There was a hubbub of chatter from the players.

"Right on, Bruiser, you show 'em!"

"Yeah, let's get going!"

"Give the girl a big hand!"

"Sock it to her, Bruiser!"

At last Bruiser growled: "OK, you bunch of nutcases – you're on!"

"Nice one, Molly," said Dessy, as they all moved towards the goalposts.

11

Shoot-Out!

There was a sense of excitement in the group that gathered in front of the goal. Mickey and Locky watched from the sidelines.

"What do you think, Mickey?" Locky asked. "Has she got a chance?" He was so proud of his granddaughter, he would have personally stepped forward to flatten Bruiser if he thought he could get away with it.

"She's got more than a chance," said Mickey. "Molly's a natural. If she keeps her nerve and concentrates, she'll sail through the contest."

Molly was indeed feeling nervous. Locky, Brendan and Dessy, and Mickey too really seemed to believe in her. She mustn't let them down. She looked across at the pair on the sidelines and smiled. Mickey gave her the thumbs-up sign.

"OK, lads," said Rick the Captain, "I mean, lads *and* Molly, of course. Let's get the rules straight for a start. So there's no room for argument, each of the team will shoot in turn, first at one goalie and then at the other. We'll play on until one of them is two saves ahead, and that makes them the winner. Everyone agreed?"

"No problem," said Bruiser. "It shouldn't take long." He smiled a nasty smile at Molly.

"OK with you, Molly?"

"Sure, Rick."

"Who's going to go first?" asked Brendan.

"*I* will, of course," growled Bruiser. "I'm the goalie, aren't I?"

"For the moment, Bruiser," Dessy grinned.

Bruiser glared at him.

Molly smiled and said: "Go ahead, Bruiser. Be my guest."

"Proper order!" Bruiser stepped into the goalmouth and the others cleared the area around the penalty spot.

"I'll take the first shot," said Rick, putting the ball down on the spot. "Ready, Bruiser?"

Bruiser was crouching down, shifting from foot to foot. "Ready!"

Rick took a few paces back, then moved forward and launched a firm kick towards the right-hand side of the net. Bruiser jumped and caught it, then raised one fist in the air in triumph.

"Right on, Bruiser, you've got 'em licked!" said one of his cronies.

Bruiser threw the ball back to Rick, and stood aside as Molly stepped into the goalmouth.

"You can do it, Molly!" said Brendan.

But Molly wasn't so sure. It was one thing to play around in her own yard, diving and jumping in front of the painted goalmouth. But now she was in the spotlight, and battling to show off her skills in front of her friends – *and* enemies! She remembered Mickey's advice: concentrate, keep focussed, ignore everything but the ball coming at you. She stared at Rick who was standing a little way back from the ball on the penalty spot.

"Ready, Molly?" asked Rick.

"Ready!"

Rick ran towards the ball and kicked. This time it went towards the left-hand side of the net, much lower than the last one. Molly dived forward and scooped it up, and rolled forward on the ground. She heard cheers and clapping from Brendan and Dessy, and from some of the other players, as well as from Locky and Mickey at the side of the pitch. She looked over to them, and saw Mickey smiling and giving the thumbs-up sign again.

"One All!" said Rick. "Back you come, Bruiser."

Bruiser stepped back into the goalmouth, looking sullen. He seemed to be wondering if this was going to be harder than he had imagined. Molly went over to Brendan and Dessy, who slapped her on the back.

This time one of Bruiser's fawning friends was going to take the kick. He gave the ball a light tap with his foot and it scuttled along the ground. Bruiser stepped forward and picked it up easily, then threw it in the air.

"He's playing pat-ball," said Brendan.

"I bet he won't give a wimpish kick like that to Molly," said Dessy.

"No way!" said Brendan.

Molly moved forward and took up her position in the goalmouth.

She heard Bruiser say to his mate: "Give it all you've got!"

Molly could see Bruiser's pal look at her menacingly as he moved back more than ten paces to take the kick. He ran forward and launched the ball high and straight towards her, with as much force as he could. It was heading for the top of the net. Molly leaped up and got her fingertips to it, flicking it back over the bar.

"Great save, Molly!" said Rick. "Two All!"

"Whose side are you on?" grumbled Bruiser.

"May the best person win!" Rick replied.

The contest went on, with Bruiser and Molly making saves alternately, until the score reached Five All.

"OK, why don't we all take a five-minute break?" said Rick.

"This could go on all night," Bruiser whinged. "Why don't we declare it a draw, and let things stay as they were?"

"With you as the goalie, I suppose?" Brendan was sarcastic.

"Of course."

Rick disagreed. "No, it's not over – if *you're* happy to go on, Molly?"

"Delighted," said Molly.

She went across to Brendan and Dessy, and started doing some stretching exercises.

"You're doing great, Molly." said Brendan.

"Fantastic!" Dessy agreed.

"I hope so," said Molly, "but it's not over yet."

Bruiser moved back into the goalmouth, and Rick gave the ball to the next player, a boy called Joe, who happened to be in Bruiser's fan club. Molly wasn't surprised to see him tap the ball gently towards the goal, where Bruiser scooped it up with ease and raised a fist in the air in triumph.

When Molly stepped into the goalmouth, she was ready for Joe to do his worst. She was right. He made a run, looking as if he was aiming at the right-hand side of the goal. Molly was ready, leaning to the right. But at the last moment, Joe switched to his other foot and the ball came hurtling to Molly's left. She quickly leaped that way, and got her hands to the ball, but it slipped through her fingers and crashed into the back of the net. There were cheers from Bruiser's supporters.

Rick said: "Six Five to Bruiser!"

Molly threw the ball back to him, and this time he passed it to Gary. Molly went across to Brendan and Dessy.

"Tough luck, Molly," said Brendan, "but keep your nerve. You know you're better than he is."

"Not so far." Molly was frowning.

"Don't worry," said Dessy. "You can do it."

From the sidelines, Mickey gave the thumbs-up sign, and Locky put his fist in the air. Molly wasn't sure if he meant it as a good-luck sign for her, or a wish to punch Bruiser.

"Ready, Bruiser?" Gary asked.

"Ready!"

Gary took a short run, and flicked the ball high and to the left. Bruiser jumped, but the ball slipped past him, just beside the post, and into the net. There were cheers from the anti-Bruiser faction, and from Brendan, Dessy, Mickey and Locky.

Molly stepped forward and Gary took the shot. This time she caught the ball firmly.

"Six All!" cried Rick.

Grumpily, Bruiser stepped back into the goalmouth.

The failed save seemed to have rattled him. He just managed to save the next one, and Molly saved hers, but at the next kick Bruiser fumbled and dropped the ball, which trickled into the goal.

Molly made her save, and the excitement grew. Bruiser was stamping about in the goalmouth in a rage. When the next ball came, he lunged at it in fury, and missed it completely.

There were cheers and a few groans, as Rick cried: "Eight Six! Molly's the winner!"

Most of the team came forward to congratulate her with Brendan and Dessy, while Locky and Mickey applauded from the sidelines.

Rick shook her hand and said: "Welcome to the Ballygandon Giants, Molly!" There was another cheer, then Rick said: "Don't forget, team, we're here to practise. Step into the goal, Molly."

"You can practise without *me!*" Bruiser snarled, stomping away towards the changing-room shed. After a few paces he turned and said to a couple of his mates: "Well, aren't you coming too?"

His former allies either looked away or shook their heads. One said: "Sorry, Bruiser. We want to be on the team."

Bruiser gave a curse.

"Language, Bruiser!" Brendan laughed, as Molly took her place in goal.

*   *   *

There were great celebrations at the evening meal. There

were lashings of sausages and rashers and chips, and Molly's mother had made one of her special trifles. She had told Locky to stop off in the town to buy a big iced cake, and Brendan made a model of a goal on top of it with three long candles and some fishing net.

"Thanks a lot, Mam," said Molly.

"You deserve it, pet," said her mother. "Congratulations again!"

"We'll clear up here," said Brendan. "Won't we, Dessy?"

"Oh – yes, of course," said Dessy in some surprise.

"Thanks," said Molly's mother.

"We'll go in and watch the telly," said her father, with a yawn.

"Well, some of us will, anyway," her mother smiled. "Are you coming, Locky?"

"No, thanks, Maureen love. I must be getting back to Horseshoe House. I'll see you tomorrow."

"Goodnight then. Don't stay up too late, all of you." Molly's mother and father went into the sitting-room and shut the door.

"We'll get this done quickly," said Molly. "Then we must make our plans."

"Yes, indeed," said Locky.

"Do you really have to go, Grandpa?" asked Brendan.

"Well . . ." Locky hesitated.

"There's a spare bed in my room – you're welcome to use that," said Mickey.

"Great. Thanks!"

As he started to pass the dishes over, Mickey asked: "What are these plans you've got to make?"

Brendan, Molly and Dessy looked at one another, and at Locky, who gave a nod.

Brendan said quietly: "Mickey, can you keep a secret?"

"Sure," said Mickey. "It's only fair. After all, you've kept mine."

"Right," said Brendan. "They're plans for tonight."

"Tonight?" Mickey was surprised.

"Yes," said Molly. "Plans for a Haunting!"

12

The Haunting

They told Mickey they were sure Mrs O'Rourke and Seamus would come back again tonight with a metal detector, convinced they would find the treasure somewhere in the yard.

"And what are you planning to do?" Mickey wondered. "You could be in danger if that pair turn nasty."

"They'll be too frightened to do anything except run for it, once they've seen Princess Ethna's ghost!" Molly was confident.

"The ghost in the story you told me, up at the castle?"

"The very one," said Dessy, in what he thought was a spooky voice. "*Fee, fi, fo, fum!*"

"That's not ghost-speak, you eejit," said Brendan. "It's what the giant says in *Jack and the Beanstalk!*"

"Well, it certainly frightened Jack!"

"You've lost me now," said Mickey. "Just how are you going to produce Princess Ethna's ghost?"

"I'm not just a goalkeeper, you know!" Molly made a sweeping bow. "I once played the Phantom Horseman. This time, it's a white sheet, a whitened face, and a crown, and *bingo*! Here's the Princess come back to haunt them."

"Where's your costume, Molly?" Locky wondered.

"I hid it here under the stairs." She went to a cupboard and produced a rolled-up sheet and a silvery crown. "I made the crown last year from kitchen foil when I was one of the kings in the school nativity play. Just as well I kept it."

She put it on while Brendan draped the sheet around her and said: "Hail, Princess!"

"I'll just colour my face with some chalk, and I'll be ready to haunt."

"Well, I must say your disguise works a lot better than mine did," said Mickey, stroking his piebald hair. "But as I said, you could be in danger if they suss you out. I think we should let your mother and father in on the plan."

"I love Dad to bits, but he's very cautious," said Molly. "He'd be all for alerting the Guards. Once that pair got a sight of a Guard, they'd be off like a shot."

"Even if they were caught, they would bluff it out somehow," said Locky.

"I still think it would be best to tell them," said Mickey.

Locky chipped in, "We'll do a deal, Mickey. As the adults here, you and I will position ourselves in hiding nearby – we'd be able enough for those two if they tried to start anything."

Mickey looked at Locky doubtfully. There was a pause.

Locky added: "After all, they *are* the Ballygandon Gang!"

Mickey grinned. "OK, provided we keep near the action."

"You're a star, Mickey!" said Dessy.

"Right, let's get busy," said Brendan. "It's nearly dark already."

He rummaged in his sports bag and took out a battered-looking metal cashbox which had once been black. He had smeared it with copper-coloured paint and dirt so that it looked old. He rattled it and they heard the clank of metal inside. When he opened its rusty old padlock, they saw a random collection of old screws and nails and broken metal brackets.

"They've come to detect buried treasure," he said, "and here it is!"

"Right," said Dessy, "all systems go!"

"You're not in the Space Race now, Dessy," Locky smiled.

"No," said Dessy, "just the Spook Race!"

* * *

When darkness fell and the moon was peeping out now and then from behind the clouds, everything was ready for the treasure hunters.

Locky was stationed round the corner of the house, where he could see into the yard between the house and the garage shed. Mickey was round the corner of the shed. Molly had shut Tina in the kitchen with a bowl of biscuits, and this time she had closed the window. She thought it best to be on the safe side, though she didn't expect they would bring Lonnigan this time – not after the bony 'treasure' he had discovered last night.

The Ballygandon Gang were all in the garage shed.

Brendan had buried the fake treasure under some earth and stones in the middle of the yard, then he had hurried into the garage shed to join Molly and Dessy. There was a dusty window in the shed which looked straight out on to the yard. Molly was standing behind the window, back in the shadows. Her face was chalk-white and she was draped in the sheet, with the silver crown on top of her black hair. Brendan had a tape on his recorder full of ghostly wails and groans and shrieks which they had recorded earlier in the day, to an audience of puzzled cows standing around in the field. Dessy had a torch ready to shine on Molly at the right moment. Now all they could do was wait.

* * *

It turned out to be a long wait.

After forty minutes, Mickey crept round to join the Ballygandon Gang in the garage shed. "Do you think they're really coming?" he asked.

"I'm sure they will," said Molly, but she sounded doubtful.

"Let's wait another half an hour," said Brendan. "Then we'll have another conference. How's Locky?"

"I'll see," said Mickey. He checked that there was no one in the yard, then went across to where Locky was hiding. Soon he was back in the garage shed.

"Locky's fine," he grinned. "He's sitting on the ground with his back against the wall, dozing happily."

"Let's leave him," said Molly. "He'll soon wake up when the action begins."

Mickey went out and back to his post.

They waited for another half hour. Brendan looked at his watch. He was about to suggest that they give up, when they heard the crack of a branch breaking in the wood beyond the fence. A man's voice cursed, and a woman made a shushing sound. The treasure hunters were coming!

Seamus Gallagher clambered over the fence and stumbled down on to the ground. He helped Mrs O'Rourke over, then reached back and lifted a long black bag over the fence. It looked just like the one they had seen him hiding under the bar. Sure enough, he unzipped it and drew out a machine with a long handle and a disc on the end. It looked like some kind of fancy vacuum cleaner.

The machine glinted in the moonlight. They saw the treasure hunters bending over it and fiddling with the controls. They seemed to be arguing about how it worked. Finally Seamus stood up proudly, holding on to the handle, and gave the thumbs-up sign with his other hand.

Mrs O'Rourke reached out to take the machine, but he wouldn't let go. The watchers could just hear some muttered words, then Mrs O'Rourke shrugged, and Seamus began wandering aimlessly around the yard, pushing the machine. Impatiently, Mrs O'Rourke nudged him and pointed towards the ground beside the shed. She indicated that he should push the machine up and down in straight lines.

So Seamus began at one corner of the shed and pushed the machine along beside the wall. He was right underneath the window so Molly stepped further back into the shadows, but Seamus was too busy staring at the ground to notice anything. Up and down he went, with Mrs O'Rourke hovering beside him.

The watchers thought it looked as if he was ploughing a field, or else appearing in some crazy vacuum-cleaning commercial.

After a while, Mrs O'Rourke's patience ran out. She seized hold of the handle. Seamus let go reluctantly, and she began to push it up and down the yard. She was getting near the spot where Brendan had hidden the fake treasure. Suddenly she stopped. Seamus said something, and she made a shushing gesture. They both listened, looking at the machine. Even through the window, Molly and the others could hear a faint crackling sound coming from the machine. From *his* hiding place, Mickey could hear it clearly. So could Locky, who had now woken up and was watching from the other side of the yard.

Seamus hurried over to where he had left his spade leaning against the fence. He grabbed it, and began to dig among the rocks and earth. The watchers heard the spade clang against the metal cash-box. Seamus and Mrs O'Rourke knelt down and began to scrabble in the ground. Before long Seamus held up the box, punching the air with his fist. Mrs O'Rourke took out a pocket torch and shone it. Then she took the box from Seamus and stared at it in the torchlight. She turned it from side to side and heard the rattle of the metal inside. She tried to pull the padlock open and they could hear her grunting and cursing as she strained.

Then Seamus grabbed the box and had a go, but he couldn't budge the padlock either. He put the box on the ground and was about to give it a bash with the spade, when Mrs O'Rourke restrained him. She picked up the box and pointed back towards the fence.

"They're going!" Brendan whispered. "Let's haunt!"

He switched on the tape recorder and held it just below the window, kneeling down to keep out of sight. The eerie sounds poured out, low at first and then louder. Dessy knelt down and shone the torch on Molly as she moved forward to the window, making moaning sounds and rolling her eyes.

They could see the treasure hunters stand dead still, looking around them wildly. Then they spotted the ghostly figure at the window and gazed open-mouthed at it, clutching each other. Dessy switched off the torch and Brendan turned off the tape recorder. They could see Seamus and Mrs O'Rourke let go of each other, still standing rigid with shock and staring at the window where the apparition had been.

Then they saw Mrs O'Rourke pointing a shaky finger towards the window. They could just hear her mutter: "It's her! It's her!"

"Who?" barked Seamus.

"The ghost from the castle. That princess who was murdered."

"Ridiculous!" said Seamus. "You're imagining things."

"You saw it too!"

"I saw something. It must be a trick of the light. Let's go."

Mrs O'Rourke didn't move. She stared at the box. "This is *her* treasure! Like the Ballygandon Hoard. She's trying to stop us taking it."

"Well, she's not going to. Give it here!" Seamus snatched the box.

"Let's give them a replay!" Brendan switched on the ghostly sounds again, and Dessy turned on the torch. Molly went through her moaning and eye-rolling routine again.

Mrs O'Rourke gave a long, shrill scream, then another. She made a staggering run towards the fence. Seamus grabbed the metal detector and followed, clutching the box. They began to scramble through the fence.

The Ballygandon Gang kept up the haunting act, till they could see them trampling hurriedly away through the woods. The ghostly sounds ended with a high, screeching laugh. Dessy turned off the torch and they all hugged each other and gave high-five salutes, doubled up with laughter.

They came out of the shed and were joined by Locky and Mickey with their own hugs and congratulations. By this time Molly's mother and father had finally been woken by the din and had come out into the yard, asking what on earth was going on.

"Let's all go inside and we'll explain," said Locky.

"The Ballygandon Gang put the treasure hunters to flight!" said Mickey.

"Oh, treasure hunters in the night again, is it?" said Molly's father. "What nonsense! This is some game you're all playing, though why you want to play it in the middle of the night when you should all be in bed beats me!"

"They were real treasure hunters all right," said Brendan, "and here's the proof." He picked up the spade which Seamus had abandoned. "And there's the hole where the treasure was. Luckily it was fake, as they'll find out when they finally get the box open."

Molly's father and mother led the way indoors, and Locky and Mickey followed. The Gang had their arms round each other's shoulders with Molly in the middle as they marched towards the house.

"Great acting, Molly!" said Dessy.

"And great lighting, Dessy. And Brendan, what a soundtrack! That cackling laugh right at the end was inspired!"

"That wasn't on the tape," said Brendan. "I thought it was you!"

"No, I was too busy doing my own moans."

They stopped and both looked at Dessy, who shook his head.

Molly said in a hushed voice: "Then who *was* it?"

13

Preparing for Battle

They all sat round the kitchen table drinking tea and finishing off the celebration cake, as Molly and the others told her mother and father about the adventures of the night.

"They were brilliant!" said Locky.

"They certainly were," Mickey agreed. "It was a case of Ballygandon Gang – Four, Treasure Hunters – Nil. A famous victory, just like it will be at the Cup Match on Saturday."

"We should really tell you off for taking such risks," said Molly's father.

"But we're not going to, are we?" her mother smiled.

"No, but I do think we should tell the Guards tomorrow. After all, that pair of crooks were breaking in to our place, and doing deliberate damage."

Locky said: "That's true, but when what they've found out about Seamus and the dumping gets known, the Guards will have a much bigger case against him."

"That's the story your father's following up, isn't it,

Brendan?" said Molly's mother. "He's due to come down here tomorrow to tie it all up. Let's wait and ask him what he thinks."

"Right," said Molly's father. "He'll know how to tackle the problem. Now, it's off to bed for you young ones."

"For the lot of us, you mean," said Locky.

As they went upstairs, Brendan whispered: "We've got another problem to solve. Let's have a planning meeting now."

They all went into Brendan and Dessy's room.

"What problem, Brendan?" Dessy whispered.

"He means the laugh we heard," said Molly.

"Exactly. It certainly wasn't on the tape. Are you sure it wasn't one of you?"

"No way."

They looked at one another.

Brendan said: "Perhaps, Molly, you weren't the only Princess Ethna lurking around tonight!"

"You mean she was trying to help us?"

"Maybe. It seems fantastic, but there've been other times when we've had mysterious kinds of help – strange messages, and unexplained happenings."

"Let's go up to the castle tomorrow – we might get some sort of clue there."

* * *

The three of them were up in the ruined castle early in the morning. Locky had gone back to Horseshoe House and Mickey was on his exercise walk. It was a windy day, with the clouds sailing across the sun. The ruined walls looked stark against the sky. They went through the courtyard to where the tower stood. Molly and Brendan climbed the stairway and looked out of the window slit. They could see the road they had followed to the hidden quarry entrance, but there were no trucks today.

"I'm sure Seamus has hidden them all at the quarry," said Brendan, "holding on to them until he gets more money from Damian."

"From what we overheard, I doubt if he's going to get it."

"Maybe we should go up to the quarry and see if the trucks are there."

"Good idea. We could go in your father's car like we did before."

"We'll ask him when he comes this evening. But there won't be time to go tomorrow, there's the big match. We'll go the next day, if Damian hasn't found the trucks by then."

They went back down the stairs.

Dessy said: "Any news?"

"No sign of any trucks on the road," said Brendan, "and no clue about the haunting either."

"Anyway, there's something we should do," said Molly, "even if it seems a bit silly."

She called up the stairs: "If you're there, Princess, and it *was* you helping us, we'd like to say *thanks a lot!*"

She smiled rather sheepishly at the others. It might have been an illusion, but they thought they heard a rustle like wind whistling through the tower.

"Well, we'll just have to dig for the treasure ourselves," said Dessy. "At least they left us a spade."

"I wonder where it can be, if it's there at all," said Brendan. "Your mother and father won't be too keen on us digging up the whole yard. If only we had a clue."

There was a beeping sound.

"That's my mobile." Brendan took the mobile out of his pocket. "It says there's a text."

"Who's it from?"

"I don't know, the screen says *'withheld'*. That means it's from an unlisted number. The message just says *'well'*."

"Nothing else?"

"No, I'm scrolling down. That's all."

"Does it mean everything is OK?" said Dessy. "That's a pretty boring message. What idiot sent that?"

"Wait!" said Molly. "What if it's a message from Princess Ethna? We did come here hoping for a clue."

"And she did send us messages by computer before," said Brendan.

"Yes, she did!" said Molly. "It must be her!"

"So I guess she's telling us we're doing well?" said Brendan.

"Or maybe it means we should look for a well," Molly suggested. "But where? There's certainly no well at our place. There's not even one in the town."

"It's a mystery all right," said Brendan.

*　*　*

That evening Brendan's father told them he had been researching the activities of Damian J O'Regan.

"He runs a building company with a number of projects in

different parts of the country, mainly quite up-market housing developments like the one in the brochure. They seem to be above-board as far as I've been able to find out, though a couple of them are in places where agricultural land was re-zoned for building. That's the sort of situation where the tribunals have sometimes found councillors were bribed to vote for the rezoning."

"Has Damian J done any of that?" asked Mickey.

"If he has, no one has found out yet."

"Well, we certainly know he's paid over money for illegal dumping," said Brendan. "I've got the proof in pictures."

"Yes, I've been trying to track down Mr O'Regan, but he's an elusive character, never calls back when I leave messages. I'm going to go to that new estate tomorrow and see if I can find him."

"You won't miss the match, will you, Dad? Molly's our new star!"

"I wouldn't miss it for anything. Maybe I'll write it up for the sports page!"

* * *

They spent the next morning practising in the yard in front of the painted goalmouth. Then an hour before the two o'clock kick-off, Locky drove them down to the pitch. They were already togged out, and did some trial runs and kicks, as other members of the team began to join them.

They saw Brendan's father arrive, and went over to him as he got out of his car.

"Well, I caught up with Mr O'Regan all right," he said,

"but he wasn't helpful at all, or even polite. He denied he'd had anything to do with illegal dumping, and said if he had paid Seamus anything, it was simply to keep his trucks in the pub yard."

"A likely story!" said Brendan.

"Yes, indeed. But he was certainly taken aback when I confronted him. He was all bluster and scornful denials. I'm sure he's not telling the truth."

"Maybe we'll get more proof when we go to the quarry again," said Molly.

"Maybe, but that will have to wait till tomorrow – right now, there are more important things happening."

"Like victory for the Ballygandon Giants!" said Brendan. "And here comes the opposition!"

A blue coach was coming towards them down the road. It parked just behind Brendan's father's car, near where they were standing. The door opened and the Killbreen Cowboys team came tumbling out, roaring and cheering as they ran on to the pitch.

Molly knew many of them from the local school.

"Hiya, Molly!" said one tall boy with a mop of blond hair. "How's it going?"

"Just grand, Jason."

"Are the Giants ready for a wipe-out today?"

"No way, Jason. You'll be surprised!" She smiled as she thought just *how* surprised they would be when they saw her in goal!

A shambling figure followed the team out of the coach. It was Seamus Gallagher. He certainly didn't look like a man who had suddenly come into a fortune. He glared at the

Ballygandon Gang, perhaps wondering how much they might know about last night's treasure-hunting escapade. From his disgruntled expression, they realised he must have got Brendan's box open and found the worthless contents.

A small green car drew up and parked behind the coach. A wiry, fit-looking man got out. He was dressed all in black – in sweater, shorts and long socks.

"That's Jack Arnold, the referee," said Molly.

Jack Arnold waved. "Hi, Molly! I see the gang's all here. But where are your folks?"

"They'll be along soon. They wouldn't miss it."

"Well, good luck to you all, I hope it's a great game."

"Jack, can I have a word?" Seamus walked over towards the referee.

"Sure, Seamus. Are the Cowboys ready to ride the range?"

"They'll trample all over them," said Seamus, "but I just wanted to ask you something."

"Ask away."

"In private." Seamus indicated Jack's car.

"OK."

They walked to the car and got in.

"What's all that about?" Mickey wondered.

"I'm not sure, but I think we should find out," said Molly. "Follow me, Mickey."

She went to the edge of the pitch with Mickey following, his hood up. They mingled with a few of the spectators who were gathering on the sidelines, then doubled back so that they were well behind Jack Arnold's car.

"Crouch down," said Molly. "We'll creep along behind the fence till we're just beside where the car is."

Soon they were in position. They listened carefully, and were just able to hear Seamus say: "Believe me, Jack, I'll make it worth your while. Killbreen has to win."

"It's not fair, Seamus," said Jack.

"Who said the world was fair? Think of what you could do with the cash. All it needs is the odd doubtful decision to go in our favour. An offside here, a foul there. The occasional yellow card . . ."

"It's against all my principles, Seamus."

"Money isn't against anybody's principles."

"I'm saying nothing, Seamus."

"And I'm certainly saying nothing. It's what you do or don't do that matters. I'll see you right, I mean it. Enjoy the game!" Seamus got out of the car and walked away towards the pitch.

Jack Arnold sat on in the car for a short while.

"We've got to stop this," whispered Mickey. "I'm not having you lose because of a crooked ref."

"What are you going to do?"

"Tell him who I am!"

"But, Mickey . . . "

Before Molly could say any more, Mickey had stepped over the fence and opened the driver's door. Jack Arnold looked up in surprise.

"Stay where you are, Jack," said Mickey, kneeling down beside him.

"Who on earth are you?"

Mickey pulled back his hood and grinned. "Recognise me now?"

Jack Arnold stared in astonishment. "Mickey Mascarpone!"

"The very same."

"What are you doing here?"

"I've come to see fair play."

"What do you mean?" Jack looked uneasy.

"I overheard your little chat with our friend Seamus."

"I wasn't going to do it!" Jack said firmly.

"I hope you weren't, but just in case it crosses your mind, I'll be watching the game, and believe me, I can spot a bent referee from two playing fields away. If I see even a whiff of a biased decision, I'll be on to the powers-that-be in football in a couple of minutes, and you'll never referee again."

"Like I said, Mickey, I wasn't going to do it."

"I'm sure you weren't. But I've a favour to ask too – not the same as Seamus's."

"What's that?"

"I'd be grateful if you didn't tell anyone who I am. I'm a friend of Molly and her family, you see, and I'm here recovering from an injury, and keeping clear of the tabloids too."

"It's a deal. I've been a fan of yours from way back. It's great to meet you." He held out his hand.

Mickey shook it. "Good to meet *you* too, Jack. I hope it will be a great game. And by the way, this is the Giants' new goalie!"

He indicated Molly who waved and said: "Hi!"

Jack Arnold got out of the car, stunned. He couldn't think of anything to say, so he simply shook hands with Molly and smiled.

14

Disasters and Discoveries

There were roars and cheers from the spectators as the referee and the two linesmen ran out on to the pitch, followed by the teams. The Ballygandon Giants were in their red strips, the Killbreen Cowboys in yellow and black. There must have been at least three hundred spectators lined up around the playing field. They were mainly families and friends of the players, and so they were cheering passionately for one side or the other.

The players ran around the pitch, warming up by kicking balls to each other and running up and down the field. After ten minutes, Jack Arnold blew his whistle and looked at his watch. The two captains came to meet him in the middle of the pitch, and a coin was flipped. The Giants won the toss. Rick the Captain looked up at the sky, where black clouds were drifting fast in the wind. It was a threatening sky and he was afraid they'd soon be playing in the rain. He decided to play with the wind behind them, blowing away from the changing-room end, so he pointed that way and the teams began to take their positions.

There were exclamations of surprise from the crowd as they saw Molly take her place in goal. Molly's friends were delighted, and surged round her with congratulations. Some of the Cowboys' team came up to the referee, pointing at Molly and beginning to argue that girls weren't allowed to play. But Jack Arnold had checked the rules too, and he simply shook his head and told them there was no problem.

The Cowboys were annoyed, but they had to put up with it. Some of them laughed, thinking this would be a walkover. Others just shrugged. Seamus Gallagher glowered from the sidelines. Bruiser Callaghan glared at Molly from his new position at left back – he had, of course, come back to the team, humiliated and still furious.

"Let's make a peace pact, Bruiser," called Molly, "at least till after the game!"

Bruiser just grunted and turned away, as the whistle blew for the kick-off.

* * *

Rick flicked the ball quickly to Brendan on his left and he made a run down the field, dodging two of the Cowboys before passing the ball across to Gary on the wing. He made a slanting shot at goal but the goalie dived across and pushed it past the post for a corner. Rick took the corner but the ball was blocked by two of the opposition, and off they went speedily down the field.

Molly saw the play moving towards her, and her heart

began to beat very fast. Supposing all her practising in the yard and all the help from Mickey had been in vain, and she failed at her first attempt at a save? She remembered Mickey's advice: *Concentrate, focus, eyes on the ball, and that's all!*

She crouched down, waiting. A high cross came over from the left wing, and the Cowboys' tall striker jumped to head it. The ball came hard at Molly, head height and to her left. Deftly she jumped and caught it, dodged past the striker and booted it to Rick in the centre of the field.

A huge cheer went up from the Giants' supporters, and Molly's friends and fans shrieked with delight. Another move began towards the Cowboys' goal. Molly felt like collapsing in relief, but instead she grinned and raised her fist in the air, looking towards where her family and Mickey stood on the sidelines, just beside the corner flag. They were all hugging one another, and Mickey raised his own fist in an answering salute. Her team-mates nearby gave her the thumbs-up, except for Bruiser, who ran past her and remarked: "Easy one!"

Molly simply laughed. "Thanks, Bruiser!"

She had passed her first test.

Ten minutes passed, with play flowing up and down. Once, when one of the Cowboys' team stumbled and fell near where Seamus was standing, they saw Seamus shout something at Jack Arnold the referee, and point towards the player, who was getting up totally unhurt, and running back to join the game. Jack Arnold simply ignored him.

"That's a relief. It looks like the ref was telling the truth," said Mickey. "There's no way that was a foul."

"It's just as well it isn't Seamus with the whistle," said Locky.

Play continued. The Cowboys saved two shots at goal, and

Molly saved a second one. As she kicked the ball forward, she felt a heavy drop of rain on her head, then several more. Soon the rain was coming down in a steady downpour. Even though they were soaking wet, the teams played on, as the ground got increasingly squelchy and people were slipping and sliding. The spectators huddled under umbrellas and pulled down their hats. Some got into their cars for shelter. But Molly's group stood their ground, as they watched her still alert in the goalmouth and completely ignoring the rain.

The play was coming towards her. She was afraid that even though she wore gloves she wouldn't be able to hold the slippery ball. It looked sodden and heavy as it was passed to the Cowboys' striker just in front of the goalmouth and he launched a high kick straight towards Molly. She jumped with her fists clenched and punched it up into the air and away from the goal.

She heard the cheers, which were soon blotted out by a mighty clap of thunder. The rain poured down in a deluge so heavy that the players could hardly see the far end of the field. There was a flash of lightning and another thunderclap, closer this time. It was followed straight away by a number of shrill blasts on the whistle by the referee. He stood in the middle of the pitch, waving his arms in the air.

He shouted: "Stop the game! Stop the game! Take cover!"

The teams hesitated, looking bewildered. The referee shouted again, but his words were drowned by a truly deafening thunderclap. He pointed off the field, and stood his ground while the players ran and squelched their way towards the shelter of the changing-room shed.

*   *   *

The air in the crowded changing room was steaming from the wet togs of the players jammed into the place. Some of the Giants and Cowboys were arguing about who had the upper hand when the game was stopped.

The referee at the door clapped his hands for quiet, and the chatter petered out.

"I'm sorry I had to stop the game, but with that storm I had no choice. What's more, the pitch is getting so waterlogged there's no way we could have any more play today. Even tomorrow, I doubt if the pitch will be playable."

"I'm sure *ours* will be!" It was the voice of Seamus Gallagher.

The referee looked at him suspiciously. "What are you saying, Seamus?"

"Our pitch at Killbreen is on higher, rocky ground, and it drains quickly. I'm sure we could stage the replay there tomorrow."

"What's he up to?" Brendan whispered to Molly.

"I don't know but, if it's anything fishy, Mickey will be there to keep an eye on things."

"It would be good to play tomorrow," said Dessy. "We're on a roll now, so let's keep on rolling!"

The referee was talking to Seamus and to the two team captains. Then he called out to the crowd: "The captains and I have made a decision. If the Killbreen pitch is dry enough tomorrow, we'll hold the replay there."

There were cheers and applause, and cries of: "Giants forever!" and "Come on, Cowboys!"

Outside, the rain was still pounding down as Molly,

Brendan and Dessy made their way to join the others, looking forward to drying out at home.

*   *   *

"You were all great," said Mickey, as they sat in the kitchen, dry and warm and well fed. "Go on playing like that tomorrow, and you'll have them well and truly beaten."

"Hey, there," said Dessy. "What does a Scottish referee do when he wants to stop play?"

"What, Dessy?" Brendan asked dutifully.

"He blows the *thistle!*"

"Why don't you go jump in a loch?" said Brendan.

"I think the rain's stopped," said Molly, looking out of the window into the back yard. "Hey, what's Tina up to?"

"She looks as if she's digging," said Brendan, "just where I buried the fake treasure."

"It must be a big hole," said Dessy, "Her tail is about all I can see."

"Let's take a look." Molly led the others outside and they went across to Tina.

"She surely couldn't have dug a hole that big!" said Brendan. "You don't suppose Mrs O'Rourke came back while we were all at the match?"

They looked down. The hole was indeed a big one, nearly two metres across. Tina was standing on one of the rubbly slopes, scrabbling to keep her footing on the loose stones.

"She might slip down into it!" Molly was alarmed. "Tina, here, Tina!" She produced a biscuit from her pocket and held it out. Tina clambered up the slope and grabbed it, while Molly took hold of her collar.

They all looked down. There seemed to be a dark round space below, circled by regular stones.

"The rain must have dislodged some of the stones and they've slipped down into that hole. I'll take a look." Brendan began to slither down the slope.

"Brendan, be careful, hold on to this." Mickey took the handle of the spade which the treasure-hunters had left behind. He held it out, and Brendan held the shovel end while he slid a bit further down till he was able to look right into the hole.

"It's all black in there," he said. "It could go very deep." He picked up a small stone and threw it into the hole. There was silence for a few seconds, then a faint splash from down below.

"I know what it must be," said Brendan. "We've discovered a well!"

Then he remembered the mystery text message with the single word 'well'. This must be where the treasure was hidden!

15

Fishing for Treasure

Molly and Dessy remembered the message too.

"This is it!" Molly exclaimed. "That's what the message meant!"

"What message is that?" Mickey was puzzled.

They told him about the time they were up in the castle, and got the message on Brendan's mobile. They also told him who they thought it might have come from. If Mickey was doubtful about their explanation, he didn't show it.

"We need a clue," he said, "and that's the only one we've got. So let's get busy!"

"I'll get the big torch from the shed," said Molly.

"Get some rope too, if you can."

* * *

Luckily Molly's father was the kind of store-owner who believed in keeping a huge range of different things in stock, just in case people might need them. Molly's mother was always saying: "We really should get rid of some of that clutter!"

Fortunately her father would mutter agreement, and then do nothing. It often turned out that a customer would ask for something unusual, and it would be unearthed from the piles of stuff in the shed. As her father produced it in triumph, her mother would smile and say: "OK, you win!"

It was ages since anyone had asked for a coil of sturdy rope, but in case they did, it was there in a corner of the shed, under a box of assorted car brake lamps.

Molly pulled it out, found the torch and brought them outside.

"Brilliant!" Mickey was delighted.

Molly grinned. "As my father would say, 'I knew that would come in useful!'"

Mickey explained his plan. He would tie the rope round his waist, and while the rest of them held on to the other end, he would go down the slope and take a look into the well.

"I think I should do it," said Molly. "I'm lighter than the rest of you – there'd be less risk of loosening the stones and sliding down."

"We don't want to lose you, Molly," said Dessie. "Imagine them singing,

Ding Dong Bell,
Molly's in the well!

Let me do it instead, I'm about the same weight as you are."

"We don't want to lose you either, Dessy," said Brendan. "We need your jokes! Well, some of them. Let *me* go!"

Reluctantly Mickey agreed that his weight could be a problem, so he suggested they have a lottery. "Whoever says a number nearest to the one I write down gets to go down the slope."

He wrote down a number on the palm of his hand. The others guessed.

"Two!"

"Forty-five!"

"Eleven – like a football team!"

Mickey smiled. "Brendan's spot-on, and that's exactly why I chose it!" said Mickey, opening his palm to show the number 11.

Soon Brendan had the rope tied round his waist and began to go slowly down the slope, while Mickey and the others hung onto the other end, leaning backwards to take the strain. The tumbled stones scrunched and slipped, and one or two slid down and fell into the well. They heard an echoing splash as the stones hit the water.

Soon Brendan was kneeling on the edge of the circular hole, on the flat stones that surrounded it. He peered down into the blackness, and switched on the torch. He pointed it at the curved sides, which looked smooth and slimy, then directed the beam further down. Eventually he could see it reflecting back at him in the water. It was a long way down, and there was no way of knowing how deep the water was.

He called up to the others, telling them what he could see.

"I could try going down on the end of the rope," he suggested.

"It's too risky," said Mickey, "and anyway, we don't know if there's actually any treasure down there at all."

Brendan was sure there must be. After all, the message had been right so far. He took the mobile out of his pocket, hoping there might be another message. But there was nothing. He glanced down into the well. To his surprise, he saw a faint light down in the depths – and the torch wasn't even on!

He called up to the others: "I can see something, down in the well!"

"The Creature from the Deep!" cried Dessy.

"Quiet, Dessy," said Mickey. "What can you see, Brendan?"

Brendan leaned over and peered in. Way down at the bottom, he could see a faint purple glow in the water. It seemed to come from some circular object, about the width of a football, but hollow in the centre. The light from whatever it was began to glow brighter and then fade, then glow again in a slow regular rhythm. Brendan gazed, hypnotised. Then suddenly the light went out. He grabbed the torch and shone it down. Once more, all he could see was its reflection in the water.

"There's something there all right!" he called. "Can you haul me up?"

* * *

They discussed what the object could possibly be.

"A bicycle tyre?"

"Much smaller."

"A kid's hoop?"

"A belt?"

Then Molly said excitedly: "Maybe it's a necklace? That would be real treasure!"

"It was a proper circle," said Brendan. "Wouldn't a necklace have fallen in more of a jumble?"

"A coronet, that's it!" cried Molly. "Just like a princess might wear!"

"Sounds like pretty fancy gear," Dessy smiled. "Do you think it would suit me?"

Molly ignored him. "It sounds exactly the sort of royal jewellery Princess Ethna might have worn on her head."

"What do you think made it glow?" Mickey wondered. "It wouldn't be radioactive, would it?"

"If it is, surely the light wouldn't fade up and down like that, and then go out altogether?"

"I guess not. So where do you think the light came from?"

"Some kinds of fish are luminous," said Dessy.

"Phosphorescence, they call it." Brendan was proud of his marine knowledge.

"Whatever!" said Dessy.

"It can't be that, anyway!" Molly was impatient. "It wouldn't fade on and off. No, I think it's a signal to help us find it."

"A signal from who?" Mickey was baffled.

"From the same sender as the text message," said Molly.

Brendan and Dessy nodded agreement.

Mickey looked at the three of them. What strange fantasies his young friends had! He decided it was best not to argue. Strange things did happen, and he certainly had no rational explanation to offer. "Well, whatever made it glow, I think we should fish it out and find what it is."

"One of us will have to go down," said Brendan.

"No, it's much too dangerous." Mickey was firm. "I

couldn't let you do it, certainly not without telling your parents."

"They wouldn't allow it in a month of Sundays!" said Molly.

"Suppose we got a ladder?" Dessy suggested.

Brendan shook his head. "I don't think there'd be room for a ladder and a person, certainly not a grown-up person."

"Not even with a rope ladder?"

"I still don't think they'd fit," said Brendan. "Someone might get jammed halfway down."

"I've got it!" cried Molly. "Why didn't I think of it before?"

"Tell us, Molly."

"Remember what Mickey said about *fishing* it out? I'll go and get the rods!"

* * *

Molly stood at the top of the slope, holding a fishing rod. Brendan was back at the edge of the well, trying to guide the line while he held the torch with his other hand.

The circular object had begun to glow faintly again. Several times he thought it was hooked, but the line came up empty.

"I know the feeling," said Dessy ruefully.

Next time, Molly felt a defnite pull on the line, and started reeling it in.

"You've got it!" Brendan shouted. "Here it comes! Yes, take it easy, I can see it. It's above the water now. Slowly, slowly. It looks just like you said, a circle, but it's stopped glowing now. It's a kind of grey-green colour."

117

"So it's not gold or silver after all!" Dessy was gloomy.

"Amazing what a bit of polishing might do!" Molly was optimistic. She went on reeling in the line slowly.

"Got it!" cried Brendan, seizing the object as it appeared above the edge of the well.

"Careful!" Mickey gave a sharp tug on the rope as Brendan looked like toppling in. He regained his balance and held up the circular object in the air.

"The treasure!" he shouted triumphantly.

The others cheered and clapped, and patted Molly on the back. Brendan heard the mobile in his pocket give a buzz.

"We'll haul you up, Brendan," said Mickey.

"Wait a moment!" He took the mobile out of his pocket and looked at the screen. There was a text message of just one word: *"YES!!!"*

16

Cups and Coronets

Back at the kitchen table, they all stood round gazing at the circular object. It definitely looked like the kind of coronet royalty might wear. It might well have come originally from the Ballygandon Hoard discovered up in the castle. Right now it didn't look up to much. It was covered in slime and muck from lying so long in the bottom of the well.

Molly touched it gingerly and said: "I think we should clean it up, to see if we can see what it's really made of. We'd feel like real eejits if we boasted about finding treasure and it turned out to be a bit of old scrap iron."

Molly's mother got out the cloth she used for cleaning cutlery. She began to rub at the coronet gently, and gradually the coating of muck began to come off. There was a small patch of glinting metal to be seen.

"It looks like gold all right!" said Locky.

"Sure does, pardner," said Dessy, in a fake American

accent. "I remember my time in them old Gold Rush Days, we could tell a piece of gold at fifty paces."

Soon, the whole crown was clean. It was certainly gold.

"Try it on, Molly!" Brendan was excited.

"I don't think I should . . ."

"Go on. It can't do it any harm."

Carefully Molly put the little crown on her head.

"Hey, that's cool!" said Mickey.

Molly had a strange feeling, wearing what must surely have been a coronet belonging to Princess Ethna. Suddenly it felt very cold on her head, and she shivered. She took it off and put it back on the table.

Just then Brendan's father arrived back, grumbling about the elusive Damian J O'Regan, who had failed to keep an appointment with him. But he forgot such whingeing when they showed him the treasure they'd found.

"You're amazing!" he exclaimed. "Every time I turn around, you unearth a new story. This could be a really big one. I'll phone my archaeologist friend Gemma. She came down once before to help us. She'll be really keen to hear about this."

"I can take a picture of it and send it up the line to her computer," said Brendan.

"Great! Let's do it!"

* * *

Half an hour later, Brendan's father was able to tell them that his friend, Gemma the expert, was very excited about the find.

"She thinks it might well be the real thing, and part of the original Ballygandon Hoard. She's travelling down here tomorrow to take a look at it. If she says it's the genuine article, I'll write the story up for the paper. With pictures of the finders, of course!"

"It's just as well Seamus and Mrs O'Rourke don't know we've found it," Molly smiled, "or they'd probably come and burgle us to try and get it."

"I'll put it in the safe anyway," said her father.

"Good idea," said Dessy, "just to be on the *safe* side!"

* * *

When Mickey came back from his exercise walk the next morning, he told them his leg seemed one hundred per cent fit again. He would soon be able to get back to playing football.

"It's a shame you can't play for the Ballygandon Giants today!" said Brendan.

"I think people might spot that I wasn't quite the right age," Mickey grinned. "Besides, you don't need me on the team to win. You've got all the talent you need."

"Will you have to let them know you're fit again straight-away?" Molly wondered.

"No, I'll wait a couple of days. I need to test the leg with a few more walks. Well, that's my story anyway. Really, I want to stay on as long as I can. It's a lot more fun here than it is at home!"

"We'll miss you, Mickey," said Molly's mother.

There was a chorus of agreement from everyone.

"I'll miss you all too," said Mickey, "but I'll come back for a visit whenever I can. And then I'd be happy to have the odd practice game with the Giants!"

"Game ball!" said Dessy. "We can call the team Michael Cheddar and the Big Cheeses!"

* * *

The atmosphere at the Killbreen football ground was building up. A great crowd of supporters had come over from Ballygandon to cheer their side on. Rival chants and songs filled the air, as the two teams ran about the pitch, warming up.

When Jack Arnold the referee arrived, they saw Seamus make his way over to him. They couldn't hear what was said, but after a few brief words, Seamus was shaking his fist, and they saw the referee turn abruptly and walk away, leaving Seamus fuming.

"Looks like he made him an offer he *did* refuse!" said Dessy.

When the whistle went for the start of the match, a roar went up from the spectators. Molly's own fans were clustered at the back of the goal, urging her on and now and then shouting "*Girls for goals! Girls for goals!*" They erupted in even louder screams and shouts when Molly saved her first goal.

The play flowed up and down the field, with several shots saved at both ends. Then the Ballygandon team made a slick movement which ended with Brendan making a short pass to the striker, who angled the ball with a firm kick past the goalie.

Deafening cheers came from the Ballygandon supporters, as the players did high-fives and punched their fists in the air.

Another five minutes, and the whistle shrilled for half-time.

The teams gathered in their huddles, with congratulations from Rick the Captain to all of the Ballygandon players.

Molly and Brendan went across to where Mickey and Locky and the rest of the family were standing on the sidelines. They added their congratulations.

"Keep it up, Molly. You're doing just great!" said Mickey. "Let's hope you won't have too much to do in the second half."

But Molly was soon kept busy as the Killbreen Cowboys made desperate attempts to even the score. Finally their striker dodged and weaved past the defenders and launched a hard kick to the left side of the goalmouth. Molly got her hands to it but the ball was travelling at such a fierce pace she just couldn't hold it. She shook her head sadly as she picked it up and threw it back to the Killbreen striker. It was their turn for celebrations now, as they ran back up the field. The score was One All!

It stayed that way until five minutes before the end of the second half. Then, after a brilliant save from Molly, she ran forward and booted the ball well up the field to Rick. He zigzagged down the pitch, beating player after player, and was just inside the box when he looked as if he was about to pass the ball to his right. The goalie moved that way, but instead Rick directed the ball straight towards the goal and past him. It crashed into the back of the net as a mighty roar went up from the spectators.

Seamus looked as if he was about to explode with rage. He began shouting at his own team and cursing the referee. The game went on at a hectic pace, as the Killbreen Cowboys tried again and again to hit home another goal. But Molly was able for them, leaping and diving to make some great saves, until at last a long blast of the whistle from Jack Arnold signalled that the game was over.

There was pandemonium, as the Ballygandon supporters swarmed on to the field and crowded round the team. At one point they hoisted Molly up on their shoulders and marched around. They were just about to let her down when she called down to Brendan: "Look, over there!"

From her vantage point above the crowds she saw Seamus Gallagher on the sidelines, having an argument with another man. It wasn't the referee this time, but none other than Damian J O'Regan. They saw Seamus hold out his hand, demanding money. Damian J slapped it away and waved to someone at the end of the field. A burly man in a baseball cap came lumbering towards him. Seamus looked scared. He turned and made a dash for his van parked a little distance away. They saw him climb in and speed away.

Damian J and his tough-looking sidekick were running too, towards the sleek car they had seen him in before. It was parked further away, but as soon as they were in it, they were speeding after Seamus.

"We must follow them!" cried Brendan. "I bet Seamus is heading for the quarry. This could be our chance to nail him once and for all."

They told the team they'd join the celebrations later, then ran across to Brendan's father, who was all for joining in the chase. Before long the Ballygandon Gang, with Locky, were all crammed into his car and making their way after the others, towards the quarry road.

17

Terrors and Triumphs

They could just see Damian J's car ahead, though Seamus was out of sight by now. They were indeed making for the road that led to the hidden entrance to the quarry. When their own car reached the wooden gate, they found it had been left open. Seamus was certainly in a hurry!

Soon they were nearing the stretch of road where the hedge with the hidden entrance was. Brendan's father stopped the car.

"We'll keep our distance for the moment," he said. "If we get too close we could be in danger."

"I'd say Seamus is the one in danger," said Molly. "Damian J looks as if he means business."

Brendan's father produced a pair of binoculars and trained them on the road ahead. "I can see O'Regan's car," he said. "It's approaching the place where the hidden entrance is. But there's no sign of the van."

"He's probably driven in already," said Brendan.

"Well, now O'Regan's stopped near the entrance, and he and the big bloke are getting out. It looks as if Seamus has left the door ajar. O'Regan is peering through the gap. Now he's beckoning to his mate. They've both slipped in through the entrance."

"Let's get after them," said Molly. "We can sneak inside and hide like we did before, and see what happens."

"OK, we'll give it a try."

He drove past the parked car and round the corner where they had parked before, out of sight.

"It's best if we don't all go," said Brendan's father. "Locky, could you stay with Dessy and keep an eye on the gate. I'll go in with Mickey, Brendan and Molly."

"Just my luck," said Dessy. "We'll miss all the fun."

"I doubt if *fun* will be quite the word for it!"

The three of them went to the gap where the disguised gate was open enough for them to peer in. They crept in and followed the road to the top of the slope, then dashed across and hid behind the upturned wagon. No one spotted them – they were too busy.

"We were right," whispered Brendan. "This is where Seamus hid the trucks."

They could see three trucks lined up in a row, with Seamus's van nearby. The backs of the trucks were towards the quarry. Damian J and his mate were standing beside one of them, shouting and waving at the driver. Seamus was at the wheel. He drove towards the pair, and Molly thought he meant to run them over. But they jumped aside, and Seamus stopped. He put the truck into reverse.

"Stop! Stop, you fool!" shouted Damian J, shaking his fist,

as slowly Seamus backed the truck towards the edge of the quarry.

Molly and the others could see that he was laughing.

"He's crazy!" cried Molly. "He's going to drive back over the edge!"

They watched in horror as the truck moved slowly backwards down the slope. It began to gather speed, slipping and sliding on the muddy ground. Suddenly, the driver's door opened and Seamus jumped out. He was just in time. The truck slithered back, and tumbled over the edge of the quarry. There was a crash and a crunch of metal, and a cloud of dust rose from the quarry.

"We must call the Guards!" said Brendan's father urgently. "This is really serious!" Brendan punched out the number on his mobile. His father explained the situation to Guard Emma Delaney at the station, who said they'd be there right away.

They saw Seamus standing at the edge of the quarry, laughing as he looked over the edge at the wrecked truck, and then back at his enemies. Damian J and his mate were striding towards him, menacingly. As the burly man went to grab Seamus, he dodged aside, and the man fell flat, only just saving himself from hurtling over the edge.

Seamus ran to the next truck and started to climb into the driver's seat. Damian J grasped the door and tried to hold it open, but Seamus slammed it shut, right on his fingers. There was a scream of pain as Damian J clutched his hand and roared, bent double and staggering about. The burly man had scrambled to his feet, and rushed over to him, smeared with mud. Damian J pointed at the truck, and the man ran towards it. He was too late.

Once more, Seamus was backing towards the edge of the quarry. The rest of them could only watch as the truck went back further and further down the muddy slope. Again, Seamus jumped out just in time, and turned to watch the truck slide back and turn over as it fell into the quarry with a crash.

The burly man ran over to him and grabbed him by the shoulders. He slammed him to the ground, and the two of them wrestled and punched at each other in the mud.

"They're sliding down!" Molly cried. "They'll go over the edge!"

Damian J rushed forward and stretched his hand out. His mate grabbed it, but Damian J lost his balance and fell down. It looked as if all three of them would soon slide into the quarry.

"We've got to help them!" said Brendan's father, and the four of them ran out from their hiding-place. Mickey grabbed Damian J's other wrist, and dug his heels in to get a foothold. The others grabbed him and he began to pull, and so did Molly, Brendan and his father. Gradually Damian J slid and scrambled up the bank, still holding on to his mate and Seamus, locked in their struggle. Finally they were all far enough from the edge to be able to get to their feet and stagger to safety. They collapsed on the ground, just as a police siren screeched, and Emma Delaney and two other Guards rushed in at the hedge gate, followed by Locky and Dessy.

As the Guards moved towards Seamus and the others, Dessy said happily: "You're nicked!"

* * *

Brendan's father made a big splash in the paper with his story of the illegal dumping and the battle at the quarry. Even more sensational was his account of the finding of the treasure from the Ballygandon Hoard, which had been authenticated as genuine by his archaeologist friend, Gemma.

There was a big celebration for the Ballygandon Giants when the Cup was presented, and Rick the Captain in his speech made special mention of Molly's part in their victory. There were huge cheers at that, and more cries of "Girls for goals!" from Molly's fans.

They had a farewell party for Mickey at lunch-time two days later. There was a cake with *GOOD LUCK, MICKEY!* written on it in red icing by Molly's mother. They gave him a Ballygandon Giants shirt as a souvenir.

Mickey thanked them all for the wonderful time they'd given him, and produced a big square gift-wrapped parcel. There was a card on it which said:

> *To the brilliant Ballygandon Gang*
> *With all my thanks and good wishes*
> *From Mickey Mascarpone.*

"You open it, Molly," said Brendan.

Molly peeled off the paper to reveal a cardboard box. She opened the lid and took out a brand-new white football. On it was written a message of good luck to the Ballygandon Giants, and Mickey's signature.

* * *

At the station, there were hugs and handshakes and high-fives as Mickey said goodbye.

"I'll be back as soon as I can," he said, "to see the fabulous Ballygandon Gang! And what a great gang you are – a bit crazy, of course, with all your ideas about messages from the Other World or whatever, but great all the same!"

Molly, Brendan and Dessy smiled at each other.

"Good luck, Mickey," said Molly. "We'll be watching all your matches."

"Great, and, as soon as you can come, I'll bring you over to see one for real!"

*   *   *

They all waved and shouted their goodbyes as the train moved off. Mickey kept waving from the window until the train rounded a corner and was out of sight. Then he sat back in his corner seat, facing the front of the train. The road out of Ballygandon ran parallel to the railway track for a couple of kilometres. Mickey looked down at it, remembering all the good times he'd had. Then his eyes widened in disbelief.

There was a sign beside the road saying:

> *Ballygandon wishes you a safe journey.*
> *Come back soon!*

Underneath the words he thought he saw a further message, in glowing purple letters that flashed on and off:

> *Good luck, Mickey!*

There was a symbol like a crown underneath, and on it the letter *E*.

Mickey stared and blinked, but in a couple of seconds the train had passed the sign. He closed his eyes but he could still see the sign blinking at him in his head. He shook himself and opened his eyes.

It must have been some trick of the light . . . Surely it must . . . ?!

The End

Also published by poolbeg.com

THE DEADLY CAMERA

GORDON SNELL

There are big celebrations at the Harbour for the brand new pleasure boat, *The Merry Midas*, and the Ballygandon Gang go to join the fun. Brendan is showing off his new digital camera to his cousin Molly and their friend Dessy, when suddenly through a cabin window he sees a strange sight. The boat's captain is secretly passing a wad of banknotes to a politician – **CLICK!** Brendan's camera has caught the scene!

This picture leads to hair-raising adventures, as the captain's henchmen pursue the Ballygandon Gang to try and snatch the camera. Through hiding-places on boats, in caves and in a haunted castle, the chase goes on. The Gang uncover sinister crimes, while thieves double-cross each other and will stop at nothing to get hold of the glittering loot. Will the gang evade capture in time to expose the *deadly truth* the camera reveals?

ISBN 1-84223-241-X

Also published by poolbeg.com

Fear at the Festival

GORDON SNELL

The Ballygandon Gang
are on the run!

A festival is planned and Molly, Brendan and Dessy,
the Ballygandon gang, are teeming with
bright ideas! Imagine their dismay when the
villainous Seamus Gallagher and his partner-in-crime
Mrs O'Rourke win the right to run the festival! It's
clear that they plan on making a nice fat profit for
themselves! Then the disco location, Mrs O'Rourke's
old barn, burns to the ground! Suspicion falls on the
Gang and they go on the run, finding an unexpected
ally in Raven the pop-star who has been invited to
sing at the festival. And, as always, the spirit of the
legendary Princess Ethna is close at hand in their
hour of need . . .

ISBN 1-84223-109-X